The taste of apple

James Laidler

The taste of apple

Winner of the Interactive Press '2010 Best New Book Award'
Judges Comments:

"The judges had no problem awarding Best First Book to this accomplished verse novel. The text is a memoir/history with strong political commentary. The text is accompanied by assorted audio tracks to be played as the reader moves through the novel, and the music itself is varied in scope.

Mature in vision and evocative emotionally, this is page-turning verse novel that should find a wide audience. The Taste of Apple is about turning the soil of life's hard garden. With flair for character and setting, Laidler goes to the core of adolescence; that painful negotiation of class, culture and family relations. This is a polished vision, a story of heart told through a language rich for the senses. Accompanied by lush audio tracks, Laidler emerges as both a talented writer and spoken word artist. An impressive debut that is ripe for the picking."

The audio aspect of this work was made in collaboration with Don Stewart. Stewart is a musician, composer, producer and recording engineer from country Victoria. He worked closely with the author in composing and producing the music for this hybrid work. Scan the code below to listen to the audio tracks for this novel on Spotify.

2nd Edition published:

January 2021

1st Edition published in March 2010 by:

IP Digital
an imprint of IP (Interactive Publications Pty Ltd)
Treetop Studio • 9 Kuhler Court
Carindale, Queensland, Australia 4152

Printed in 12 pt Cochin on 14 pt Cochin.

National Library of Australia
Cataloguing-in-Publication data:

Author: Laidler, James

Title: The Taste of Apple / James Laidler.

ISBN: 9780646832487(pbk)

Other Authors /Contributors:

Stewart, Donald James (1961-)

For
Clare Batten,
Peter Chapman
&
the people of
East Timor

*The pursuit of truth and beauty
is a sphere of activity in which we are permitted
to remain children all our lives.*
– Albert Einstein

The world will be saved by beauty.
– Fyodor Dostoyevsky

Prologue:

Age 18:
Richmond

Breathe

A tar-coated roof,
an apartment block,
Lennox Street.
I tug at the bank-issued tie
around my neck,
take off my Blundstone boots,
my faded navy socks,
and step out
towards the edge.
Folding my toes
over a corner of concrete
I balance myself,
careful not to drop my gaze
to the dizzying world
stretched out
22 stories below.

The drone of traffic
radiates up
like summer heat,
trapped for too long,
in too much concrete.

And breathe.

Far below
a river of headlights
flickers and flows
under the old railway bridge,
and along
the tapestry
of Richmond's streets.

Breathe deep,
hold it,
exhale.

I close my eyes,
stretch out my arms
and lean that little bit closer
to the brink,
closer to the margin,

closer to the rush that sometimes,
sometimes,
brings relief.

*Breathe in
deep and strong this time,
hold it.*

My eyes reopen
to a smoggy night sky
and a symphony of stars
plays for me
my own private song
and I listen.

I listen
as the week's memories
and the nameless faces
viewed through the syrupy
plastic window
of Teller 6
slowly fade away.

*Breathe out,
long and true.*

I think of Dad
living somewhere on a farm
near Colac
and pour my thoughts
into the *big saucepan's* starlit frame
to simmer and steam.

Then to the east,
from behind a wispy cloud,
five stars appear
in perfect formation.

I take my heart
—filled with the image of my Mum,
collapsed on our brown
vinyl couch,
eight floors below,
next to her overflowing ashtray—
and nail it
to the Southern Cross.

Skeleton man

The *Herald Sun* says
he died six months earlier
and all that remained
were his bones,
nothing more!

But I wonder
where they found him.
Face down
on musty, beer stained carpet;
his bones arranged
in flawless formation?
Reclined
in an armchair,
covered in mouse shit?
Or were his bones
like burnt-out match sticks,
skittled across the toilet floor?

The *Herald Sun* claims
that in the year 1999
it's a scandal!
A pensioner,
a Lithuanian,
a post World War II immigrant
living in a commission flat,
five stories
above
where I now sit.

The *Herald Sun* says
he had no family,
no friends,
and no
decent
neighbours!

But I wonder,
what a "scandal" actually is.
Is it a scandal
that I can't picture
the old man's face?

That somehow
I'm to blame?
Or is the scandal
that outside my flat
discarded syringes,
the smell of stale piss,
and walls caked with graffiti
don't make people
feel very neighbourly?

The *Herald Sun* says
that our flats on Lennox street
were built in the late 1950s
in an effort to clear out the slums
and create low-cost housing
for the poor.
Employing the "latest Swiss design"
and accommodating a thousand residents,
the flats were opened back then
to much ceremony
and applause.

The *Herald Sun* says
that the housing commission
is under pressure to house
recovering addicts,
the mentally ill,
ex-cons,
and those
fighting serious drug
and alcohol problems:
Vietnamese gangs,
Sudanese youth,
war orphans
and maybe even
ex-child soldiers.

I close the newspaper,
hurl it on the faded yellow
linoleum bench,
next to the pile
of unwashed dishes,
and wonder
to which group
I belong.

Chapter 1:

Before the fall

Age 10:
Heidelberg

Playing war

'You're dead!'
Chris Reed jabs
the barrel
of his plastic M-16
hard
into my ribcage
and raises his voice
in victory.

A rattling train
thunders over head
like artillery fire.

'Johnno,
Blake!
Hey,
over here!
The last one's
over 'ere!'

Two boys,
slightly shorter than Chris,
materialize like ghosts
from behind a picket fence
and glide
shadow-silent
into formation
beside their fearless leader.

I crouch
head bent,
inside my dugout
of rubbish bins, cardboard boxes and milk crates;
a defeated soldier.
My rifle,
an old eucalypt branch,
wilts in my fingertips,
falling to the ground
as Amy Reed,

my eight year old team mate,
trundles over from the kerbside;
a guilty look
on her face.

Chris taps his wristwatch.
'2 minutes stick-boy,
get going!' he barks.

I stare
back and forth
at Amy,
the "turncoat",
and Chris,
the "enemy".
Over and over
and over
again,
muscles tightening.

My pulse
throbs like
a burst of bullets
in my ears,
until suddenly,
I pull the pin
and words explode
from my mouth:

'Stop cheating you prick!'

And that's how I got
this scar.

The one
high above my right eye.

Chris Reed,
his henchmen,
a smashed toy gun
and a battle
by the tracks.

Seven

The Silver-Top taxi
pulls into the Austin Hospital car park
and Mum and me
climb into the back.

Waiting in the front passenger seat is Dad
who takes his eyes
off the ticking meter
and glances back
at the seven stitches laid out
above my swollen
and bruised
right eye.

'Banksia Street,' he says to the taxi driver,
returning his gaze to the meter.

As we drive down Bell street
Dad mutters something:
a question.

His words thread their way
through the wounded and silent spaces
of the taxi,
tying up my thoughts.

I press my head
against the cool glass
of the passenger window
and stare out into the darkness.

Seven stitches,
seven words:

'So what happened to the other kid?'

Blessed art thou

Steady,
sturdy,
soft,
straight hands.

Mum lights a candle
in my darkened room
and places it
under the icon of St Peter
on my desk.

Shuffling over to my bedside
she falls
feather-light
to her knees.
The smell
of flowering Jasmine
wafts through the window,
lifting me to a better place.

She dabs
at the blood-clogged
stitches
above my right eye
with a warm,
wet cloth
then places
the reddened fabric
back
into a steaming bowl of water
by her side.

Mum's left hand
enters her pocket,
returning
with rattles
and clinks.
Wrapped around her fingers:
a jangled web
of rosary beads.

The crystal edges
and silvery links
catch the flickering light;
ensnaring
my eye.

'Your name means rock,
Pedro,
just like St Peter,'
she whispers.
'You're my rock, Pedro,
don't you forget that.'

I look up
at mum's face
bathed in golden
candle light
and manage a smile.

Her lips start to move
as once tedious words
pour from her mouth
like honey.

'Hail Mary, full of grace...'

My eyes grow heavy
and my head sinks deeper
into the pillow.

'Blessed is the fruit of thy womb...'

Under my doona,
I turn on my side
and curl up
tight
into a ball.

'...pray for us sinners now.'

A wet, warm cloth
strokes
the side of my face,
wiping away my troubles.

Sleep swallows up the night.

After midnight

They're fighting
in the kitchen.
My sister Dalisay turns up the radio
in her room,
but I can still hear their voices.

'You're never here!
He needs you, John!
You're always at work,
in your shed
or at the pokies,
but never here!'

Mum speaks strange words tonight;
stranger words
than I've ever heard before.
I picture her
on her favourite kitchen stool
lighting a fresh cigarette,
fingers trembling.

Dad doesn't respond.

The flyscreen creaks open
and his measured footsteps
click, clack their way
down the garden path
towards the shed.

It's after midnight.
Dogs are barking
at the moon
and outside my window
the jasmine vine
rustles in a
dark spring breeze.

Lying in wait

'Dad's waiting for you...
in the shed.'

Mum grabs
my milk-splashed
breakfast bowl,
wipes clean the placemat
and returns to the sink,
ignoring the look of shock
on my face.

As I walk towards the shed
I double check
my shoe laces,
shirt buttons
and smile
before knocking.

'Come in Pedro,' Dad calls.

I push open the door
and step into Dad's place.

My eyes dart around.
In one corner there's a leather recliner,
coffee table
and reading lamp.
Under the lamp,
an ashtray
and a smouldering cigarette
curling wisps of smoke
up towards the roof.

To the left
is a little glass cupboard
full of spirits:
Johnnie Walker,
St Remy,
Smirnoff,
Hennessey

and right beside that
a bar fridge
purring
like a satisfied cat.

At the other end of the shed
there's a drop saw,
a work bench,
and a wall panel
covered in assorted hand tools;
each tool neatly hung
and bordered
by hand drawn lines.
And along the back wall,
there's a heavy green curtain
covering up something big.

Dad steps over to
the workbench
and looks down
at a rifle
lying on top.
The rifle's made of polished wood
        and black ice steel.

He picks it up.

The stitches
above my right eye
start to throb
as Dad swings the gun
in my direction.

The rifle

The rifle feels heavy
as Dad places it
in my hands.

'It's a .22 Calibre Winchester.
I used to go rabbiting with it
as a boy.'

Dad leads me over to the work bench
and points,

    'Place it down there
    on that long piece of pine.'

I put the rifle down
and Dad takes a pencil,
carefully tracing
its outline
onto the wood.

'You better sit down
and get comfortable,' Dad says,
pointing to the recliner.

For the next 3 hours
I watch Dad
measure,
saw,
plane,
chisel,
and sand
in silence.

I sit there dreaming of my new gun
and the look on Chris Reed's face
the next time we play war.

Mum calls for lunch,
but Dad ignores her.
He lifts the wooden rifle
up to his shoulder
and looks down
the finely sanded barrel.

'Almost finished,' he mutters.

He grabs a short length of poly pipe
from a cardboard box
and screws it
to the top of the rifle:
a sniper's scope.

I look up
with big saucer eyes
at my skilful Dad
as he runs his fingers
over the surface of his new creation
looking for faults.

'Perfect,' he says,
'perfect.'

Perfect

At lunchtime I eat everything
Mum throws down in front of me.

The wooden rifle rests on my lap
      smooth to touch. A perfect lunch.

A perfect day.

Age 15:
Heidelberg

Our old rented house

The three inch plaster crack
first started to appear
in the lounge room
when I was twelve.
For the next three years
I watched it grow,
shedding its chalky skin
like an old man with dandruff.

'Bloody trains!'
Dad steams and puffs,
the house shuddering
during breakfast.
My seventeen-year-old sister,
Dalisay
and me
sit opposite dad
at the dining table
careful not to laugh.

Dad brushes the white plaster powder
like so many pesky flies
off his navy suit,
but it's a losing battle.
A few uninvited specks
always fall
on his carefully combed hair
his porridge,
his toast,
his tie
or the packet of Peter Stuyvesant's
by his side.

Our mum, Imee,
sits statue quiet
and watches her husband
from a stool
in the kitchen.
Her long, black Filipino hair

draped over her shoulder like a heavy curtain
blocking out the light.

Once I asked mum
why she didn't make Dad's breakfast,
or lunch
for that matter.

She just stared at me for a long moment
and said,
'John doesn't like it.'

Dad's peak hour rush

The timetable never changes
after breakfast in our house.
Dalisay and me call it,
'Dad's peak hour rush.'

After stoking his boiler with porridge
Dad pulls into the kitchen
and we watch
as he prepares
his lunch for work
and loads it into his briefcase.
Mum reckons the routine
has to do with the fact
he's a draughtsman.
'He does things the best way,' she'd always say.

A thermos of black coffee.
Check!
Two sandwiches,
margarine thin,
pickles thick,
ham folded
and cut into triangles
Check!
One large red apple,
quartered,
de-cored
and glad wrapped.
Check!
Two scotch finger biscuits.
Check!
One calculator
Check!
Pens, pencils and rolled up plans.
Check!

Dad snaps the briefcase locks shut,
glances at his wrist watch
and thunders out of the kitchen

in a straight line
towards the door.

At the last moment
he turns and calls out,
'I'll be home late,
don't wait up.'

The front door slides shut,
the kitchen kettle boils,
and my mother rises from her stool
with a sudden look of relief
on her face.

'Come on Pedro,
Dalisay,
quick now,
it's time for school.'

Outside
a passing train
shakes the poor foundations
of our little rented weatherboard house
near Heidelberg station,
on the Hurstbridge line,
and my sister and me
get up slowly from our seats
ready for a new day.

Year 9 roll call

'Enrique Rodriguez?'
'Yep 'ere'
'Lucy Jackson?'
'Yes miss'
'Vijay Dhoni?'
'Yo!'
'Marco Lombardi?'
'WHAT?'
'Andrea Slokovic?'
'Not here, probably wagging, Miss!'
The classroom sniggers.
'Neima Lomac?'
'Lomac?'
The replacement teacher peers
like a prison warden
over the wall of paper on her desk.
'Lomac?'
I bump the dark shape of a girl
slumped over the desk beside me.
'She's here,' I say.
'And Pedro Ong... Ong...
Oh I'm not sure how to say this.'

'It's Ongpauco,
but that's my Mum's surname.
They were meant to change it last month.
It's Jones,
Pedro Adam Jones,' I say,
tugging at the collar
that has become a hangman's noose
around my neck.

Marco Lombardi chuckles,
swings around,
and looks me up and down.
He winks at Lucy Jackson
then pulls tight
the corners of his eyes
forming slits.
'Ong, dong, tong, fong!' he spits.

Lucy smiles.

Carrying a flame

Soon after dad leaves for work
mum pushes us out the door
with kisses and cuddles.

The front door closes dungeon tight
and walking to school
I picture mum
monsoon-dreaming:
wiping benches,
dusting photos,
cleaning basins,
cooking Kare Kare,
then dusting
over and over again —
Just the way dad likes it.

Dalisay and me walk down Bell Street
now humming with buses,
motorbikes and cars.

Before too long
we pass the old Olympic rings
strung out on rusted wire
between the Alamein Street shops.

The idea of attending
Heidelberg West High School,
nestled in the heart of Melbourne's 1956 Olympic village,
was dad's of course.
He insisted that me and my sister
walk the 20 minutes to school everyday
because unlike
the mostly white
and pricier Heidelberg College,
located three blocks
down the road,
at "Westy"
we were more likely to "blend" in.
Out at Westy, our Filipino black hair

and "tanned" skin
wouldn't matter.

In history class
Mr Swaggert teaches us
how under those rings the Prime Minister,
Sir Robert Menzies,
in January 1956 cut ribbon
and raised champagne.
Swaggert tells us,
while bouncing and prancing about
in his neatly ironed shirt,
that the village was built
to house
visiting athletes,
'from all around the world!'

Swaggert says,
'we should feel privileged!'
He says our school gymnasium,
which smells nowadays like rotting fish,
once trained the world's best
and that down Bell Street
the Olympic torch had passed
with great fanfare.

After the Games were over,
the Olympic village
was converted
into public housing,
but Swaggert never talks about that.
And the fact that West Heidelberg
has one of the poorest postcodes
and highest crime rates
in the whole of Victoria
doesn't get a mention either.

I stop after school at the Alamein street shops
and gaze up at the perfectly proportioned Olympic rings
that Swaggert says
symbolise peace and unity.
'What a fuckwit!'

Five rings.
One for Mr Swaggert,
one for me,
and one each for Dalisay, Mum and Dad.
Five misfits
jumping through hoops!

I walk home,
fists clenched,
carrying a flame.

Gifted

Mr Swaggert says
I'm bored in class
because I'm "gifted".
He tells my mum,
my maths teacher,
my English teacher,
and word of my "giftedness" spreads
throughout the student body
like an incurable cancer.

Gifted!

With a simple word
Swaggert single-handedly
doubles my homework
and makes me the target
of each and every student
with a chip on their shoulder.

'Smart arse!'
'Nerd!'
'Geek!'
My new titles get flung
around the yard,
down the corridor
and across the classroom.

At Westy,
a school big on "diversity",
I suddenly feel
like I've overstayed my welcome.
Not because of the colour of my skin,
but because I love reading,
facts,
figures
and the smell of
crisp white paper.

I spend my lunchtimes
in the school library

where Mrs Harbrow
scans,
sorts
and taps away at her keyboard.

I imagine myself as a book
lying flat on Mrs Harbrow's
squeaky returns trolley,
ready for sorting and reshelving.
A yellow hardcover book titled:

"Gifted Student: Reader Beware!"

One good thing

Despite all the bad press at school,
there is one good thing
about being called gifted —
and that's the opportunities
it brings.

Without being "gifted",
I never would have attended
John Marsden's writer's camp
in Romsey,
 where I first discovered
my passion for words
and poetry.

And without being "gifted",
I wouldn't have been
encouraged to enter
the writing competition
where one of my poems
won first prize.

That's right, first prize!

And without that,
I never would have
received the cheque in the mail
for a hundred bucks.

Yep, that's right,
a hundred bucks!

The agreement

There's an unspoken agreement
between Mum and Dad
in my house —

it's been that way forever.

Mum follows
Dad's strict rules
about cleanliness and order,
and in return,
Dad tolerates
Mum's obsession with Filipino cooking
and all things Catholic.

In our house
the lines have been drawn
in the sand
ever since I can remember.

The truce has never been broken.

And that's the way
Dad likes it.

Perfection

I find the old dusty rifle
Dad made for me when I was ten
under my bed.

My shoulder presses hard
into the rifle's butt.
The gun's tip
edges out my bedroom window.
My rage pours through the plastic scope and down
the barrel like molten lead.

'Perfect,' I whisper.

I fantasy-fire
        my bullets
into an unsuspecting neighbourhood

I spy the neighbour's noisy dog.

Blood red,
        dead!

A squawking magpie.

Puff,
        a cloud of feathers!

My school jumper hanging on the line.

Rip, tear
        thread bare!

And the lock on Dad's shed door.

I pause,
remembering.

The lock on Dad's shed...

Inside that shed
is a heavy green curtain
hiding something big!

Keeping up with the Joneses

I start to understand
why my 17 year-old sister Dalisay
never invites her friends over anymore
and why Dad
comes home late
from work
every night.

First there's mum's cooking:
oxtail Kare Kare soup,
mud brown sinigang stew
and bloated palabok noodles.
After a sesame oil fry-up,
with a south-easterly blowing,
you can smell our joint
all the way down at Heidelberg Station.

Then there's all the Catholic stuff:
rosary beads hanging on the umbrella stand,
the portrait of Jesus
in the lounge,
crucifixes dangling from walls,
and a figurine of Mary
in the kitchen.
There's even an icon of St Francis
in the toilet.
In the toilet for God's sake!

Yeah, I start to understand.

I start to understand
when Vijay comes over
for the first time
after school.
Mum sits him down at our table
and insists he has a snack.
'Crispy Pata,' she says,
placing a plate of fried and battered
meat sticks before him.

Vijay's eyes light up
and he munches away.
But the next minute
he's coughing, spluttering
and pulling out
a long, wiry hair
from halfway down his throat.

'I'm so sorry, so sorry,' Mum says,
'I thought I got all the hair off,
I'm so sorry.'
Vijay looks down
at the tasty meat stick.
A chunk of batter falls off its side
revealing a pig's trotter
underneath.

Vijay never visits again
and I start to understand.

Most of all
I start to understand
just how undesirable it can be
"keeping up
with the Joneses".

On Friday

On Friday
I arrive at school
and open my locker door.
Stuck to the inside panel
with masking tape
is the hand drawn picture
of a giant,
slobbering,
pink
pig
wallowing in mud
and eating its own shit.

Underneath the picture,
in red texta,
are the words:

U R What U Eat!

Grandma Jones

Grandma Jones
lives in a red
double-brick house,
with an English cottage garden,
in East Malvern.

On the mantelpiece
in her living room
is a sumptuous urn
containing the cremated remains
of her dead husband,
the bank manager,
Alfred Drummond Jones.

Ever since I can remember
Dad would take Dalisay and me
once a fortnight
to visit Grandma Jones.

She'd always greet us at the front door
with makeup-heavy eyes
and Palmolive words,
directing us
to the bathroom
to wash our filthy
and contaminated hands
before entering her domain.

She'd then hand
a shopping list
to Dad
who'd disappear for four long hours
while Dalisay and me
helped Grandma with chores
around the house.

I'd be put to work outside
in the neatly manicured garden
to weed,
dig,

mow
and rake.

In spring,
Grandma's heavily flowered garden
would explode with colours and smells.
But always,
always,
my attention would be drawn
to the tightly staked
rose bushes
in the front yard.

The roses,
so naturally wild, fragrant and buoyant
always seemed so diminished
in their English cottage prison,
their thorns
their only means of defence
against their warder's hands.

They would sit there
row upon row
burning in the afternoon sun
like a chain gang of inmates:
working all day
for the benefit of others,
while suffering
in their own private hell.

Waiting for Dad

With our chores complete
Dalisay and me
would wait for Dad's return,
eating ham and pickle sandwiches
in Grandma's dustless lounge room.

We'd sit
on an ugly plastic sheet
thrown over Grandma's
expensive leather sofa,
bored out of our brains.

Whenever Grandma left the room
Dalisay and me would lift the edge
of the plastic sheet
and throw
pieces of pickle and crust
down the side
of her leather cushions.

Grandma would return
oblivious to her two
half-caste grandchildren,
sitting in the corner,
like over-shaken
soft drink bottles,
trying to keep a lid
on the urge to laugh.

Inheritance

Mr Swaggert gives me a book
about this German bloke,
      Marx
who reckons religion
is the "opiate of the people".
Swaggert says "opiate"
     means "drug".
It makes me think of Mum
and the whole Catholic thing.

Dad once told me,
shaking his head,
how some young men
in the Philippines
actually "volunteer" to be crucified
every Easter:
'They take three inch nails
and drive them right through their bloody palms!'

When I ask mum about it
she starts by giving me a run down
of her life as a kid
growing up in San Fernando city.

She remembers the smells mostly:
burnt oil,
passionfruit cakes,
monsoon mud
and decay.

But she also remembers
hot, bloated nights
where plain-throated sunbirds
would line up
     as sentinels
       on tired and droopy power lines
          marshalling in the sea-salt mist.

And yes she remembers seeing
very clearly

not one,
not three
but twenty-four real life crucifixions
at Cristo Rey Mountain Park
when she was 16
and she has the photos to prove it.

A minute later and Mum returns
with a motley brown scrapbook
which she opens like an old wound;
    the faded black and white photos spilling out
        onto the floor.

The images slice into my dreams.

    I toss and turn at night;

receiving my inheritance.

In need of a sponsor

At school I type
"public crucifixion" into yahoo
and navigate my way to
to a Filipino tourism website.

There's a picture of a Filipino man
being crucified
surrounded by locals
dressed in centurion costumes.

In the background is a giant billboard
sparkly red
with white writing:

COKE IS LIFE

The caption under the photo reads:
    "Angelis Religious Tours;
take yourself to the heart of reverence."

                'That'd be bloody right,'
I laugh to myself.

A bit more searching
a webpage later
and I discover how
"Coca Cola will be soaking up the goodwill today
as the key sponsor
of the Good Friday crucifixions
in the Philippines."

I laugh again
and I can't help but wonder
if maybe
there's a sponsor out there for me
who can save me from this shit-full life.

A sponsor who can throw
a "schweppervescent" smile
my way
to bubble and fizz

and lift me out
of this yellowish white
Asian bright
wetsuit tight
pig ugly world.

A key and a ticket

Dad's shed key
hangs on a hook
by the back door
like a tasty apple
ready to be picked.

In a plastic tray below
are some unused train tickets
which Dad uses
to get himself to work.

I gently lift the shed key
from the hook
 and pocket a train ticket
 for good measure.

The key to unlock a mystery.

A ticket
just in case I get caught.

I stand at the back step
thinking through my plan;
my mind stopping all stations.

I stare at the key,
cold and brassy
in one hand
and at the train ticket

yet to be validated

in the other.

Dad's shed

Dad's at work.

I butter-slip the stolen key into the lock
twist
and click.

The shed door creaks open.

A quick look behind,
a quick swallow
and I step
phantom-like
into the unknown.

Dad's bookshelf

Dad's shed smells of linseed oil,
axle grease
and regret.

I peel back the heavy green curtain
on the back wall
to reveal:
a bookshelf.

The books are arranged,
alphabetically of course,
and browsing the titles
I suddenly realise
I've stumbled into Dad's "opium" den.

Who would've thought
Swaggert's bloody book
about Marx
would prove so on the ball.

'Fucking drugs everywhere,' I think,
my eyes starting at the letter A.

Astral Travel in the 3ʳᵈ Age
Numerology: Unlocking your potential
Search for the Holy Grail: Christianity Exposed
How to Win Friends and Influence People
The Melbourne Theosophical Society Journal, Volumes 1-10
The Secrets of Positive Thinking
Think Rich; be Rich

I spend half an hour flicking through the books
and realise Mum and Dad
have more in common
than I thought.

They both yearn, hunger, ache
and crave
for something more.

They follow a similar calendar

but live

seasons apart.

The bottom shelf

On the bottom shelf
I find a worn
and faded magazine
wedged between two heavy books.
I yank it out.

The Australasian Post,
Issue 232,
November 1978.

I turn to page three
and gasp at the model
staring back at me:
caramel eyes,
thick toffee hair,
strawberry lips
and mixing bowl tits.

I chew over
the strange discovery;
my eyes glued to the page.

Five minutes later
I'm back in my room
slipping my new trophy
underneath the mattress
praying Dad
will never
never
find out.

Dal

It's mid November
and Dalisay says
she's thinking about leaving home.

She says she's met a bloke
who rides a motorbike.

She says she's getting her nose pierced.

She says there's work
picking fruit up north
near the Murray.

Dal says crazy stuff!

She's another bloody addict
just like Mum and Dad
only she's sniffing "dreams of escape"
in search of her Holy Grail.

I leave Dalisay in the lounge room
with her secrets
thankful
I'm not a junkie like her.

The Australasian Post I

1800 PILLOW TALK

1800 CRAZY GIRL

CALL ME, CALL ME NOW!

ϖ CHERRY ϖ
Home, Hotel, Motel
ϖ Friendly Discreet Service ϖ

FORBIDDEN FRUIT ESCORTS
WHEN ONLY THE BEST WILL DO

The back pages
of Dad's *Australasian Post*
rustle back and forth
with the flick of my fingers.
My eyes prune away the boring bits
until all I'm left with
are ripe words
and juicy images.

My heart beats harder and harder.

On the back page
is a small ad
that's been circled
with a ballpoint pen.

The Filipino Bride Connection

A reputable, sophisticated service with 15
years experience.

Call 1800 973 786

I dry up inside
and the pages of the magazine
fall from my fingers
like autumn leaves
to the floor.

The Australasian Post III

Late at night
when everyone's asleep
I creep into the kitchen
in search of answers
and punch the numbers
into the phone:
                    1800 973 786
'The number you have called is not connected,
please check the number before dialling again.'

The phone pumps its pointless pulse
down the line
and I stand there
        waiting

until the beeping stops
        and the sound flat-lines.

I return to my room
and bury myself alive
                        under the doona.
 A dead heart
        A purchased start
        A number dialled
            A telephone child

    Praised be my creator!

The Australasian Post.

Mass

We sit
        as usual
in the fifth row.

Mum's all
        bent knees
            thumb-kissing
                downturned eyes
                    and whispers.
Dad?
Well Dad's just there
out of obligation
although sometimes
I reckon he
glances at the blonde
two rows back.

It's two weeks out from Christmas.
The smell of eucalyptus
is blowing through the church's side door
and a Kookaburra
is cackling outside
while Father Damian
tries to give his homily.

Father Damian ignores the laughter,
driving his sharp
vinegary words
like nails
deep into the parishioners.

I sit,
trapped and strung out,
between Mum and Dad;
                two thieves
            stealing my youth.

Mum elbows me
And I tumble back to reality
joining in with the end of the creed:

We look for the resurrection of the dead
And the life of the world to come
Amen

Christmas eve

Dalisay, Mum and me
get back late
from shopping.

There's a letter on the coffee table
and a neatly wrapped present
under the tree.

Dalisay reads the letter
staring at it
    with graveyard eyes
before handing it to me.

I stumble at the first sentence,
    "It's time for me to move on..."
Stagger at the words,
    "I'm sorry for not being
    a good husband or father."
And fall at,
    "Yours Sincerely,
        John"

my tears flowing,
    hot and salty.

Simple words.

Words even Mum would understand.

In silence

The lights
strangling
the Christmas tree
blink and burn
Red
Yellow
and
Blue

Mum returns from the kitchen
with cold glasses of milk
and a plate of shortbread biscuits;
sugar-dusted
and cut into the shape
of angels.

Dalisay looks up at Mum,
her cheeks black with mascara,
but it's me who speaks:

'Sit down, Mum
Dad's gone,
he's gone!
Why can't you just sit down?'

'Back off, Pedro,' Dal snaps.

Mum looks our way
then slumps to the couch,
defeated.
For what seems an eternity
we sit around the coffee table
in silence.

The Christmas lights
blink and burn
Red
Yellow
and
Blue

as a car alarm sounds down the street

as the milk
    turns warm
                in our glasses.

The Christmas present

Mum's staring at the floor,
Dalisay's buried her head
    into a cushion,
nobody's talking
and I can't stand it anymore.

I reach under the Christmas tree,
past the baubles, lights
         and decorations

and drag the present
back to my lap.

Dad's gift,
wrapped in red metallic paper,
sits there
laughing.

I rip and tear at its
shiny skin;
the sudden noise
waking Mum
from her trance.

She looks at the box in my hands.

'Scrabble, deluxe edition,' I mutter.

I turn the box over
and start reading aloud
the contents,
almost choking on the words.

'With its polished wooden frame,
embossed playing surface,
wooden tiles
and velvet bag,
Scrabble Deluxe
is the perfect combination
of good looks
and improved functionality.'

'Stop it Pedro,' Dalisay moans.

'Pick your letters,
rack your brains
and marvel at the built-in turntable
which allows the board
to turn easily during play.'

I stand up
and rip the lid off the box,
dumping the contents onto the coffee table.
The shortbread angels snap and crumble.
The velvet bag falling to the floor.

'It's a good present Pedro,' Mum says
trying to be diplomatic.

'How can you
say that,' I yell,
'he's a bastard!'

'Stop it,' Mum cries,
'Stop it!'

I reach down,
grab the velvet bag
and dig out
a handful of wooden letters.

'Come on then,
let's play!'

I hurl the letters at the Christmas tree,
dislodging the star on top.

'How do you spell "prick"?
How do you spell "fuckwit"?' I scream.

I scrunch up the bag
and throw it hard
against the wall.

 'How do you spell "father"?
How do you spell "son"?'

I grasp the corner of the coffee table
ready to flip it over
but Dalisay jumps up
just in time,
slapping me across the face.

'Get outta here!' she shouts.

I look at her
for a long moment
then march off to my room
and out the back door
holding my old rifle in one hand
and my stinging cheek
        in the other.

The rhythms of rage

I hold tight the barrel
and swing it like an axe.

I shatter-snap the windows,
kick, slash and hack.

I smash through the doorway
picturing his face.

My fist through the fibro
tears at his place.

I demolish his memory
and destroy all I find.

I splinter my fingers,
splinter my mind.

Rip the recliner,
I tear it apart.

I puncture the silence,
I puncture my heart.

A woman for all seasons

Strong,
sturdy,
steady,
sure hands.

Mum pushes me up against the wall
      waking me from my madness.

'Go to your room now!' she orders,
'and take these with you.'

I feel the heat in her words
and
the rosary beads
pressed deep into my palms.

I leave Dad's shed
stepping over
broken glass,
torn upholstery
and the fragments
of a finely sanded,
handcrafted
      rifle.

Holy woman

I slam shut
the bedroom door
and throw the rosary beads
on the floor.

Climbing beneath the doona
my hand reaches
under the mattress,
returning with a torch
and Dad's old, crumpled
Australasian Post.
Deep in my cotton cave
the flashlight awakens
and I unzip my fly.

Mum lights a cigarette
in the kitchen
as my hidden prayer begins:

> *Hail centrefold*
> *Full bodied, with grace*
> *The Lord is with you*
> *Blessed art thou among models*
> *And blessed is the curve of thy breast; pleasing.*
> *Holy woman*
> *Wonder of God*
> *Stay with this sinner now*
> *In the hour of my death*
> *Amen*

The torch battery runs flat.

Sleep swallows up the night.

Christmas morning

A half-dream fog
blankets me,
thicker than my doona,
as I stare
out a crack of curtain
in my bedroom.

There's a motorbike
in the driveway
conversation
in the kitchen,
and dried up blood
on my fingers.

Outside
a scalpel of sunshine
slices through the clouds
and across
my sleep-sore eyes;
jerking my head
back into
the shadows.

It's Christmas morning,
the sun's hot
and the streets
are quiet.

I slip on my clothes,
step out of my room
and walk cautiously
towards the unfamiliar voice
in the kitchen
    and the smell
of slowly roasting meat.

Ned

'This is Ned,' Dalisay says
as I step
into the kitchen.

Dreadlocked hair,
scuffed up leathers,
studded tongue,
Ramones t-shirt.
I look
at the first bloke
Dalisay ever had the guts
to bring home
and fake a grin.

Ned steps forward
hand extended.
'Good to meet you mate,
I'm sorry about...'

'Me too,' I interrupt
shaking his hand quickly,
limply
and watching his smile
dissolve before
my eyes.

Dal gives me a dirty glance
but I look straight past her
to Mum
who's standing there
dressed up for our big day
like a poorly sung
Christmas carol.

Mum looks up at me
and I search her face
for a hint of anger,
    betrayal, anything,

nothing.

For the next two hours
Mum's all tinselly words,
silvery smiles,
Christmas cheer
and cigarettes.

We sit around the table
eating the only meal
Mum ever cooks
"the Australian way"
telling each other crap-happy
bonbon jokes.

Then,
as I tear open
the last Christmas cracker,
and fit the paper hat
on my head,
Mum just looks at me
—the newly crowned
 male head
 of the family—
and without another word
stands up
and leaves;
her bedroom door
clicking shut
down the hall.

Me and Dal
sit there
adrift,
staring
at the tough,
listless meat
on our plates;

at the meat

        drowning

in gravy.

Age 16:
Heidelberg

In my darkened room

A hungry winter wind
rumbles hard
against the bedroom window
and a ripped parcel
—postmarked "Colac"—
lies discarded
on the floor.

As I sit at my desk
holding the strange gift
in my hands,
I picture Dad's face.

"PEDRO"

The gold-leafed letters
on the front cover
of the leather journal
glisten
under the lamp light.

The gift feels heavy,
too heavy.

It's the 1st of August
my 16th birthday
and three months since I last saw Dad.

I slowly open the journal
and inside the front cover
sits Dad's
elegant handwriting:

*Mum says you've been
doing it hard.
I thought this little journal
might help. I know how much
you like to write.*

Happy Birthday,

Dad

I grab a pen
and sit at my desk
for a long time, thinking.
Lost for ideas,
I flick open my dictionary
to a random page
and try to find inspiration
in the first fancy word
that appears.

Cornucopia: *an abundant, overflowing supply.*

My pen suddenly springs to life.

My Poem: Landslide

Falling
    falling
        falling,
through January
    April
        Winter
           and Spring
A year of natural disasters.
A landslide year, Dad,
of mud-slow memories
   and mistakes.

A landslide year Dad

of Mum's never-ending forms,

'Pedro, can you fill this out for me?'
she'd always ask.

Yes, that's right Dad,
a landslide of forms,
documents and decisions,

watching Mum tumble,
        bumble,
         and fumble her way
through housing commission questionnaires
Newstart Allowance protocols,
and red tape;
   with me
her only help.

A year of natural disasters, Dad,
   and a landslide year
     of waiting.

Waiting.

Seconds,
minutes,
hours,
and days.

Month upon bloody month.

Yes a landslide year
of waiting.

Ordinary time
stretched out,
a cornucopia of emptiness,
rolling,
cascading,
land-sliding down
through my life
in analogue, not digital
     grey, not technicolour
mono, not stereo, Dad!

Waiting
with Mum
for hours
on hard plastic seats.

Waiting
for the infernal red glow
of the Centrelink queue counter
to change.

Waiting,
just sitting there, Dad,
shifting and squirming in my seat,
daydreaming,
striving to remember,
yearning to forget,
waiting.

Yes, always waiting, Dad.

Waiting
in bed at night
for my insomnia to pass
and the nightmares to begin.

Waiting
for Mr Swaggert
—Do you remember him Dad?—
to get off my back
and for Year 10
to hurry up
and fucking end.

Waiting, Dad,
for a word
from Dalisay,
picking fruit
up north.

Waiting
for my life to improve,
for Mum
to smile
again
and for you
to pick up
the phone.

Holding her close

There's a brief knock
then mum's troubled face
at my bedroom door.

'What did he send you?'
she asks in a whisper.

I hold up the journal
and Mum steps in closer
for a look.

'For your writing?' she asks,
resting a hand on my back.

'Yeah, I guess so.'
I open the journal
to the first page.
'I've already made a start,
wanna hear it?'

Mum nods her head
and as I read my poem
I hear her sniffle.
A single tear falls
from her cheek
to the journal below,
sending a rivulet
of salted ink
down the page.

After a few minutes
Mum speaks,
'We loved each other once you know.
When John found me
 he was very lonely,
but I thought he was a good man, Pedro.'

'Then why did he leave?'

'I don't know.
I don't know.
All I know is we drifted apart.'

By the time I stand up
and wrap my arms
around my Mum
she's sobbing uncontrollably.

I stand there
holding her close.
Close,
like a loving son should.

School awards

The school hall is packed
and Mr Gunther,
our principal,
stands at the front of the stage
hands on hips.
The noise slowly drops
as he stands there
putting out spot fires
with a verbal spray or two.

Over at the lectern
Mr Swaggert
taps at the microphone,
'Testing, um,
is that ok?
Alright then...
welcome to our final
awards presentation of the year.
Today we are going to...'

Five minutes later
I'm daydreaming
and staring at the back
of Neima Lomac's head
in the front row.
Her tight black Sudanese curls
look like little steel springs.
I imagine reaching out
and touching them
when an elbow
from Marco Lombardi
brings me suddenly back
to earth.

'Pedro Jones,'
Mr Swaggert calls,
'Pedro Jones,
please make your way
to the front
of the stage.'

I look at
Marco Lombardi
sitting beside me,
smirking,
and my stomach lurches.
I stand slowly
and squeeze my way
down the too tight aisle.

Halfway to the stage,
Mr Swaggert starts reading out
my award:

'Pedro Jones
of 10A has won
a very special award indeed.
This award celebrates his efforts
in the MS Readathon.
Pedro managed to read
over 100 books
and raise over $300 dollars.
What an achievement!'

There's a sprinkle of applause
as I mount the stairs,
but all I feel is regret.
Regret for letting Mr Swaggert
convince me
to take part
in this stupid "extension" activity.
Most of the other kids
my age
had stopped doing the Readathon
in primary school
for God's sake!

I know his intentions were good,
and God knows
I needed the daily trips
to places like ancient Greece,
Middle Earth
and Mars.
But this?

As I stand on stage,
in front of the whole school,
I know I would
take it all back
to be anywhere
—and I mean anywhere!—
but here.

'For his efforts
Pedro has won a special family pass
to Luna Park ,' Swaggert adds.

Mr Gunther
takes my hand,
shakes it vigorously,
and presents me with a framed certificate
and my prize.

I walk back to my seat,
head downturned,
a freak
and a loser,
remembering all the reasons
why I hate teachers,
school,
and Marco Lombardi.

The family pass

I take the family pass
off my bedside table,
open a drawer
and hide it
deep down,
underneath the boxer shorts
Grandma Jones
gave me last year
for my birthday.

That night
I dream about
the clown's face
guarding the entrance
to Luna Park.
I dream about its
funeral white skin,
its big red smile,
mocking me,
daring me to enter,
and its enormous open mouth
ready and waiting
to devour me alive.

Letter of acceptance

I know Mum's got
some serious news
when she sits down
beside me
on my bed
and without speaking
hands me a letter.
I read it carefully,
taking in each word:

'...we are glad to inform you
that your application
has been successful.
One of the flats
at our Lennox Street residence
in Richmond
is now available...'

Mum's arm
wraps around my shoulder
protecting me
from the fall.

Chapter 2:

A concrete kind of life

Age 16:
Richmond

Eden Towers

With feet of clay
I step
from the taxi
onto the hard
          hot
          bitumen road.
Mum pays the driver,
who smiles unsympathetically,
while I reach
into the back seat
and throw our bags
onto the nature strip.

The taxi speeds off,
spitting stones.

Bending down,
I grab my swollen suitcase
and haul it
to the other side
of Lennox Street.

The suitcase drags behind me,
like a old piece of road kill,
as I tramp along
the boundary
of my new home.

Eden Towers
the housing commission calls it,
located smack bang
in the heart of Richmond
between two rivers:
      The Yarra River,
with its sluggish-brown waters
to the East,
      and Hoddle Street,
with its surging stream
of city traffic
to the West.

Reaching the shade
of a tired and twisted
Morton Bay fig,
I stop to catch my breath
                    and look up.
Through the branches
the silhouette
of an apartment block
        curtains
the blue sky.

The beads of perspiration
on the back of my neck
start to evaporate
as I stand there;
small,
naked
and exposed.

Eden Towers
the housing commission calls it:
a colossal man-made finger
thrust from the ground
towards the sky
        in defiance.

Eden Towers:
22 stories
and 47 years
of concrete,
steel
and pressure.

Some unknown hand

Stepping out
from under
the fig tree's canopy
and into the sunlight,
I stare up

        up

          up

at my new home
for a better look.

Standing there
paralysed
in the hot oven sun,
I wipe the sweat from my brow
and feel
my heavy clay feet
harden
in the heat.

'Come on Pedro,
everything's ok,' Mum encourages.

A cigarette lighter
scratches to life
behind me
and turning around
I see Mum's face
through the smoky haze.

Mum's smile
blows a little life
into my stiff
terracotta limbs;
just enough
to get me moving again.

I pick up my suitcase
and walk slowly
towards the automatic
sliding doors

at the base
of the building.

Waiting in the foyer
for the lift to arrive,
the smells of
urine,
beer
and human traffic
overwhelm my senses.

We ride the lift
to the fourteenth floor
and make our way to No. 3
—our new home.

Placed here by some unknown hand,
I lie awake
on my first night
picking through memories,
trying to harvest
some secret knowledge
about how I ended up here;
     here,
               in this God-forsaken place.

Sundays in the city

Staunch,
steady,
stiff,
stubborn hands.

Mum adjusts the tie
around my neck
and flicks the hair
out of my eyes.

'This is all I ever ask,'
she says,
giving me a look of warning
and money for a tram ticket,
before pushing me out the door
and towards the lift.

After six weeks
at Eden Towers
this had become
our one
weekly
ritual,
our time spent together,
our "time of bonding".

What a joke!

For mum,
our Sunday trips
to St Patrick's Cathedral
had become like a
"golden thread",
weaving in and out
of our hastily patched up lives;
holding together
the whole shebang.

For me though,
life was closer

to a tattered old garment
    on the verge of unravelling.
There was no "golden thread";
    just frayed edges,
and poorly stitched up seams.

Mum and me walk to the end of Lennox Street,
past an old drunk
muttering to an invisible friend,
    a half-eaten McDonald's cheeseburger
        left abandoned in the gutter,
  and a council worker
    in a fluoro jacket,
raking the playground sand
in search of discarded syringes.

At Victoria Parade,
we catch a No. 96 tram,
up the hill
to the Brunswick Street interchange.

A quick
two block walk
down Gisborne Street,
past some old elm trees,
and we suddenly arrive in another world.
A manicured world
of trimmed lawns and roses,
trimmed hair,
trimmed smiles
and towering bluestone walls
—St Patrick's Cathedral.

Mum and me follow the crowd
heading in
for eleven o'clock Mass.
And just outside the wrought iron gate,
that's where I see him,
    once again,

just like every other Sunday:
my neighbour,
the one from the eleventh floor,
the Asian busker with the shaven head
and smart arse smile.

He stands there,
proud and defiant,
	like a modern-day biblical prophet,
shredding his fingers
on the strings
of his tattered guitar.

He stands there,
eyes closed,
veins bulging,
throwing out his lyrics,
like barbs
at those passing by:

*'Get your motor running
Get out on the highway
Looking for adventure
Whatever comes my way
BORN TO BE WILD!'*

The busker with the smart arse smile

Waiting for the tram home
after Mass
Mum has a sudden realisation:

'You've forgotten your jacket Pedro.'
'You better go back.'
'Quick, before your ticket runs out.'
'I'll see you back home.'
'Hurry...'
'Run...'
'Run!'

Mum's anxiety-fuelled words
cause my legs
to shift into gear
and hurtle me
back down Gisborne Street
in a blur
of city sounds
and colours.

I run fast
through pedestrian crossings,
ignoring their flashing red lights
and slow rhythmic ticks.

I run fast,
my feet slapping asphalt
like aftershave applied to new-cut skin.

And I run fast,
up the stairs
to the entrance
of St Patrick's cathedral
where I stop at the top,
dropping to one knee
—breathless.

The gigantic gothic doors
guarding the now quiet building
frown down at me
as I adjust my tie,
catch my breath,
and enter.

Inside the cathedral's foyer,
I stop myself
and stare at the peculiar sight
of a beaten-up guitar case
propped up
against an old,
metal collection box.

Plastered with an unfamiliar flag and stickers,
the guitar case shouts:

'Free Xanana Gusmao!'

'Viva Timor Leste!'

'Support East Timorese
 Asylum Seekers!'

Mindful of my jacket,
I turn away from the guitar case
and continue on my way
through the foyer,
past the cathedral's gift shop
and out amongst the pews.

Reaching the fifth row,
I locate my jacket
and turn to leave
when something out of the corner of my eye
catches my attention.

Slipping silently behind a nearby pillar,
I lean out to take a closer look.

Through the filtered light
I make him out.
     The busker.
Kneeling on the floor
of a small candlelit shrine to the side.

I watch him
in secret fascination
as he slowly and carefully
runs his musical fingers
over the shrine's intricate mosaic floor.

His hands move,
back and forth,
as he mumbles to himself,
tracing the contour of each small tile
with loving precision.

His hands move,
back and forth,
strumming the cracks in the floor
like the strings of an antique guitar;
whispering his own private song
to a captive audience
of stained-glass angels,
stone statues
and me.

The long walk home

Back outside,
with an expired tram ticket
    now in my hand,
I prepare myself
for the long walk home.

 Still thinking about the busker inside the cathedral

—his dirty, shoeless feet,

his khaki army jacket—

              I step forward
    when,

all of a sudden,

a hand around my throat
    spins me around,
slamming me up
against a cold, bluestone wall.

Up Close and Personal

'You spying on me bitch?'
he yells,
squeezing my throat
  like the handle of a blacksmith's hammer. 'Answer up
or I'll beat the fucking truth out of you,
         you church-tie prick.'
'I've seen you before
and I know where ya live
—three floors above me,

         you and your fucking mother!'
'Now   tell   me   what   you   saw!'

'Come on, speak up ya dumb fuck!'

'Speak up before I beat it out of you!'

But there are no words,

    just a sudden mess of tears
  which fall
       and pool
around the busker's steel-forged fingers,
      cooling his grip,
      releasing his hold.
His head shakes.

'Shit, stop fucking crying
ya weak prick!'

'I'm n...not a weak prick,' I stammer,
wiping away my tears
and standing up a little straighter.
'And I'm not your "mate".
Maybe you're the prick!
And maybe
  I saw nothing!'
      The reckless words
  jump from my mouth

before I can catch them
and shove them back where they came from.

I stand there cowering
                in the shadows
        of my own bravado.

The busker goes quiet for a minute,
sizing me up
before speaking,
'Maybe you saw something,
maybe you didn't.
But one thing's for certain,
        "mate!",
down at the "Towers"
those tears of yours
are gonna get you fucking killed.'

The busker's unexpected words
slap me across the face
so hard,
something inside me snaps.

'You don't know me,
so why don't you just piss off!'
I shout,
hitting him square in the chest.

The busker's feet give way
and he lands on the concrete with a thud.
I stand there in shock,
bracing myself for a fight.

Fists clenched,
jaw locked,
I wait
        and wait,
            blood pumping,
                    but nothing...
The busker just sits there
on his arse
and bursts out laughing.

'That's the spirit, brother!'
he calls up to me,
extending his hand in my direction.
'Well, are you gonna help me up or wot?'

The huge wave of adrenaline
coursing through my body
slowly subsides
as I look down,
    perplexed.

After a few moments,
my hand nervously reaches down
and drags the busker to his feet.

Standing next to him,
up close and personal,
I suddenly realise he can't be much older than me.

'Sorry 'bout that. I fucking
lost the plot, didn't I?' he says,
turning our clasped palms
into a handshake
and smiling from cheek to cheek.
'I'm Juan,
Juan Lazzaro.
But everyone calls me Johnny.
Welcome to the neighbourhood.'

The long talk home

'I've got to get going,'
I say to him awkwardly,
as I stand there
    in the steeple-shade,
hands in pockets,
eyes slumped.

But Johnny just smirks
and insists on "walking",
(or should I say "talking")
me home.

It's hard to believe someone
can transform themselves so quickly,
but that's just what Johnny does.
One minute he's a dangerous animal;
the next he's a
bubbly and chatty pest.

As we walk,
Johnny's face
is a big screen TV,
lit up.
His hands,
a tangle of antenna
gesturing here
                there
    and everywhere
in search of reception. His mouth
a speaker
crackling static.

I try to tune into
his mad mutterings,
but it's difficult.
Johnny's words are
                on   the   move...
    his thoughts hard to follow.
They flicker,

flash,
and jump
from one subject to the next.

    And yet...

              by the end of the first block
something happens;

           I relax...
    chill-out...

     let go...
It's as though I'm back home
with a remote control in my hand,
channel-surfing after midnight.

I walk beside him
in a daze,
soaking up the snippets
of his life;
    tired
but totally unable
to pull myself away
from his
strange
    incandescent
          glow.

Johnny says

Johnny says
my 'tie's a health hazard'
and I should
'take it off before it hurts somebody.'

Johnny says
the last time he went to Mass
was 'six years ago
in East Timor.'

Johnny says
he 'refuses' to go to Mass
because he's 'protesting.'

Johnny says
he's an 'asylum seeker.'

Johnny says a lot of stuff.

Johnny says
his Dad was arrested and tortured
in East Timor
for belonging
to the wrong political party.

Johnny says
his Dad had to sell
everything he owned
to get him to Australia.

Johnny says
his Dad was put in prison
when he tried to leave East Timor.

Johnny says a lot of stuff.

Johnny says
he lives with his uncle
and aunty now.

Johnny says
his uncle's a 'white Australian prick'
and that if it wasn't
for the free accommodation
and his East Timorese Aunty,
he'd be outta there!

Johnny says a lot of stuff.

Johnny says
life would suck without music.

Johnny says
Dylan's his favourite
followed by Nirvana.

Johnny says,
'all you need is three chords
and the truth
and that's the way I busk!'

Johnny says
you can make easy money
by busking
and that I should try it sometime.

Yeah, Johnny says a lot of stuff.

Johnny says
a single mother overdosed on smack
in our flats five months ago
and 'it made the fucking news!'

Johnny says
he knew the mother
and that her body was found
on the living room floor
while her baby was found
dead in the cot.

Johnny says
the baby girl
took two long days to die

and that they found her
'with her dummy
still in her mouth!'

Johnny says
he sees the baby
in his dreams at night:
'sucking on that fucking dummy
'til blue in the face!'

Johnny says a lot of stuff.

Johnny says
I need to steer clear of
the Suddie gangs
in the area.

Johnny says,
'those Wu-tang, Sudanese pricks hate Asians,
so watch ya back, brother —
 there's a fucking war going on.'

Johnny says
There was a huge fight
the other day
down at North Richmond Station:
'Pipes,
chains
knives,
you name it!
One Vietnamese kid got stabbed in the fucking neck!'

Johnny says a lot of stuff.

Johnny says
rules are made for breaking,
music for making
government forms for faking,
and risks for taking.

There's no doubt about it,
Johnny says a lot of stuff.

And Johnny also says
that what I 'saw' earlier
in St Patrick's cathedral
was none of my 'bloody business!'

Johnny then apologises to me
 for talking
so rudely.

Actually, Johnny says
'sorry'
all the time!

'Shit, sorry 'bout talkin' so much mate!'

'Sorry, I'm gettin' a bit worked up, aren't I?'

'Sorry, did you just say somethin', brother?'

We stop
at the last set of traffic lights,
and Johnny suddenly realises
that I am trying to say something.
He looks over at me
and lets me repeat my question.

 'Where's your Mother?' I ask.

Johnny goes quiet,
takes some Drum out of his top pocket
and rolls himself a smoke.
We stand at the intersection in silence,
waiting for the lights to change:

 'She's dead.'

The little man turns green.
Johnny lights up,
draws back hard
and keeps walking.
I follow
as long tendrils of smoke
swing out behind him

and the tobacco burns
slowly,
right down to the stub.

Finally, Johnny flicks the cigarette butt
into the gutter
and turns to face me.
The words he speaks
burn and smoulder
like the tip of his discarded smoke.

'She Died in Santa Cruz
in 1991,
but you've probably never heard of that, have you?
Dili massacre?
Murdering Indonesians!'

Johnny looks at me
hard in the face
his eyes aflame,
then suddenly smiles,
shakes his head
and slaps me on the back.

 'Shit mate,
 I'm sorry 'bout that!'

There's no doubt about it,
Johnny says a lot of stuff.

Troubled

Sweating in the midday sun,
down sleepy city streets,
stepping over cracks,
feet sodden with aches,
he walks with me;
my new
quick-talking companion.

Is he my friend, then?
This chameleon, this shaken up mixture
of happiness and anger, this overspill
of beer
dripping in steps beside me?

By the look of him,
he's troubled.
His endless chatter a virus,
    catching.
And I can spell *danger.*

But still, why can't I tell him to go away?

I love the petrol stench of his words
and the way they linger
on my clothing,
mind
and lips.

They're flammable!

        yet...

    as I walk

and Johnny talks

new life

    into the seized-up cylinders
of my heart,

the simple question remains:

Why can't I tell him to go away?

Why can't I tell him

to just piss off?

Parting company

We stop in the shadows
of the flats
and Johnny says goodbye.

'My name's Pedro by the way, Johnny.
Thought you might like to know that,'
I say with a smirk
as he steps away.

Johnny swings around
and looks me up and down.

I watch
as a big thick smile
spreads across
his face
like melted butter on toast,
quickly soaking up
my wise-crack.

'Of course it is, brother.
Shit, I heard your Mother say
your name weeks ago.'

Johnny shakes his head
and leaves,
this time laughing to himself
as I stand there
completely "shut down".

All alone now,
I look back
in the direction of St Patrick's Cathedral,
trying in vain
to sift through
the jigsawed mess
of information about Johnny
now littering
the city's streets.

I stand there
as a gentle breeze caresses my cheek
picturing the places on our journey
where Johnny's life
now lies,
    laid out in footsteps.

Miss January

She's wearing a see through number
as usual,
but my mouth's already watering
just from the thought of her.

It's ten minutes past midnight
and my sweaty fingers
tear through her plastic dressing,
anxious to expose
what's beneath:
the curve of her hips,
the pink of her lips,
the rise
        and fall of her air-brushed tits.

Her deep sultry eyes
connect with mine,
drawing me in,
sending a shiver
down my spine.
She stares at me
in that teasing way
and I struggle to resist her allure.

Miss January.

The first penthouse pet of 1998
sits spread eagled before me
on my bed
and a big part of me,
Dad's half I suppose,
says she's a beauty.

The other part of me,
Mum's half,
tells me she's barely worth the $7.95
I handed over
to the young female store attendant
at the Seven Eleven;
and definitely not worth the embarrassment,
or the shame.

After I'm done
I place the tube of sorbolene cream
discreetly under my bed
and step over to my desk.

I quietly remove
the desk's bottom drawer
and in the cavity below
place Miss January
with her friends:
Miss April,
Miss July
and the girls from Dad's old
Australasian Posts.

Back in bed
I toss and turn,
unable to sleep.

Questions.

Wave upon wave
roll through my head,
pummelling me,
        over and over again.

I toss and turn,
caught in a whitewash of bed sheets
        and a sea of
questions:

'Why do I feel so bad?'

'Why do I feel dirty?'

'Does this mean I'm wicked?'

'Why can't I say no?'

'Why do I feel so trapped?'

'What would Mum think?'

'Why can't I resist?'

'Why does it make me feel
so alone?'

Resting in Pieces

I sit on the plastic sheet
thrown over Grandma's expensive sofa
listening to Mum and Grandma argue
in the kitchen.

'I need his new address Florence,' Mum says.
'The kids haven't seen him since he left.'

'Look Imee, it's not my problem,' Grandma replies.
'Maybe if you'd been a better wife
this wouldn't have happened.'

I grit my teeth
and try to tune out,
but it's no good.
Grandma's words sizzle and hiss.
Their talk gets
louder and louder.

I stand up,
walk over to the mantle piece
and look up at the fine China urn
containing Grandpa Jones' cremated remains.

'You're in my house
and should remember your manners, Imee,'
Grandma says scornfully,
'I won't have you badger me
with demands!'

I read the little plaque
on the bottom of the urn
as Mum's pleads her case
in the kitchen.

The plaque reads:

ALFRED DRUMMOND JONES
REST IN PEACE

'Maybe you should be leaving,'
Grandma says all of a sudden.

Her harsh words
lift me out of my daze.
And with those words
I take the urn down,
open the lid
and in a fit of anger,
spread the remains of Grandpa
all over Grandma's Plush Berber rug.

The world becomes
a blur of heat
as I stamp Grandpa
deep into the rug
 with the soles of my feet.

It's only when Grandma
walks into the lounge room
five minutes later
and screams,
dropping the vase of flowers in her hands,
that I come to my senses.

'No!
Alfred!
What have you done!
What have you done!'

Russian Doll

I've never been
in this much trouble
before.

I've been sent to the guest room
while Mum tries
to repair the damage
with Grandma.

Mum and Grandma
are on their hands and knees
in the lounge room
with a dust pan and brush
and a plastic bag.

I picture them sharing the impossible task
of trying to scoop up
Grandpa
from the carpet;
thankful, at least,
that I can't hear them bickering anymore.

I sit near
a pile of antique teddy bears
on Grandma's hard spare bed.
Beside me,
on the bed side table,
is an intricately painted
Russian doll.
I think Dad use to call it a Matryoshka doll.
I lift it to my lap.

I remember playing with it
when I was a young child.
I remember my fascination
as each wooden doll
would split
neatly in half
to reveal another identical doll
beneath.

I start opening up the dolls
layer by layer
like an onion.

As I split open the third doll,
I pause
at the sound of Mum
starting up the vacuum
in the lounge room.

I imagine Grandma
slumped on the clear plastic sheet
thrown over her expensive sofa,
watching Mum work,
wet with tears for Grandpa
and hatred for me.

The vacuum does its duty.
I hear the tinkle-tap
of particles as they wiz up
the tubing.

Layer upon layer.

I open the fourth doll
and start to wonder which bits of Grandpa
are being lost forever:
an ear perhaps,
his hands,
or maybe even that dimple
on his once proud jaw.

Layer upon layer,
just like an onion.

Layer upon layer.
I sit on the hard spare bed
opening up the little painted dolls
searching for an end
to all this hollowness.

Just like Mum

Mum and me
catch the bus home
from Grandma's house
in silence.

I've been grounded for a week
and Mum doesn't speak to me once.
But at least I know she's happy
to now have Dad's address
on the slip of paper in her purse.

In the end,
I think Grandma gave it to her
just to get rid of us.

The bus rumbles
around a corner
and I put my hand in my pocket
to grab the smooth shape
of the little Russian doll hiding there.

The final layer.
The final doll.

I look at my Mum sitting quietly beside me
and run my fingers over the little doll's
hard varnished surface.

Maybe I took the doll
because it reminded me of Mum.

She's just like this little doll.

She might be small.

She might seem insignificant.

But at least she can't be split in two
like the other dolls.

She's solid.

Solid the whole way through.

Neighbours

Although I don't know her name,

I know her.

Separated
by a thin single wall,
of plasterboard and steel,
I know her.

I know her in
the Doosh! Doosh! Doosh!
          of her stereo
    at night,
   in the crackle of her laughter,
in the filth of her words,
and the boom of her husband's voice.

I know her
in the sizzle of fat
from her kitchen
and in the burnt meat stink
that leaches
under our locked front door.

I know her
in the rattle and clink
of their empty stubbies
as they're carried
in plastic bags
to the bins
fourteen floors below.

And I know her
when their drinking ends
and their shouting begins.

Yes, I know her
in the creak of their furniture,
        the smash of their plates,
the slap

of his open palm on her cheek,
and the punch
of my mum's fingers
on the telephone:

"000"

"Neighbours", Channel Ten
always reminds us,

'Everybody needs good neighbours.

Neighbours,
should be there for one another.

That's when good neighbours
become good friends.'

Everybody needs good neighbours

The chain on our front door snaps tight
as big fat fingers
push through the crack.

I can smell the beer.

'Keep ya fucking nose
outta our business!' he screams.

I dodge the glob of spit
sailing towards my face
then run my shoulder
hard into the door.

His fingers slip back
as the door slams shut
and I collapse in a heap
on the floor.

There's one last kick at our door
    from his boot
before his heavy footsteps
retreat down the hall.

Mum sits
frozen on the couch
with the telephone on her lap,
                beeping.
It's 9 o'clock at night
and looking past Mum
I see
the setting summer sun
through the lounge room window
as it coughs up
a molasses of murdered red
on the city's skyline.

Getting to my feet,
I walk slowly
towards the sticky,

dripping,
bloodied light
and rest my palms against the glass.

The red covers everything:
the buildings,
the sky,
the events of this night,
and the promise of tomorrow.

I stand there
fighting back tears,
watching the setting
summer sun

        slowly bleed out
into

   darkness.

Should be there for one another.

'This is Mr Santiago, Pedro,' Mum says
as I step through the front door.

There's a walking frame by the TV
and an old man
with an oily comb-over
sitting on our brown vinyl couch.

I stand there
squeeze out a smile
and put down my journal.

'Not another one,' I think to myself.
Yesterday,
it had been Mrs Albanese
from the third floor.
Three days before that,
old Mrs Tran.
Last week it had been Sister McKenzie
from the Good Shepherd.
And a fortnight ago, Evie Gutteres,
a little five-year-old girl from down the hall.
I recall how surprised I'd been the day
Evie got dumped on us.
The little girl's mother
showed up at our front door
all worked up about a 'doctor's appointment'
she couldn't afford to miss.

I ended up playing with Evie
for the whole afternoon
in the playground.

I walk into the kitchen,
fill a glass of water
and start to think about
all the people Mum had managed to befriend
in the last month at Eden Towers.

All the people she had met
in the elevator,
the corridors,
or the communal laundry.

All the people she could now greet
with a smile,
polite bow
or friendly word.

And all the people she now kept supplied in
hot cups of steamy green tea,
long conversations,
baked cassava biscuits
and offers of practical help.

'It's the Filipino way,'
she would always say.

I take a sip of water
and actually manage a grin,
recalling how much better
Mum had seemed lately.
Between her new part-time job
working at Van Nguyen's Asian Grocery Store
on Victoria Parade,
early morning Mass,
and her regular volunteer work
two nights a week
with the Matthew Talbot Soup Van,
Mum almost seemed happy now.

Last week,
Mum even responded to a poster
calling for new residents to join
the community garden project
located at the base of the flats.

'I need to see things
grow around here,' she tried to explain to me.

And yet,
there were still those other days.

The days I hated.

The shithouse days when I'd get back from school
to find mum curled up in a ball
on the couch
unable to speak;
lying there all day long

with her rosary beads limp in hand,
staring at the framed photo
of Dalisay, Dad and me on the coffee table.

On those days
dirty unwashed dishes would pile up
on the yellow linoleum bench
and for dinner
I'd end up eating baked beans from a can
in the half-dark of my bedroom.

I refill my glass and wander back
through the lounge room
and towards my bedroom,
but as soon as I enter
Mum raises her voice.

'Mr Santiago needs help with his shopping Pedro,'
she says.

'What's that?' I ask,
not fully catching her words.

'Mr Santiago's too old
to carry his shopping Pedro.
I think you
can help him, yes?' she asks.

I look down at the little man
sitting on our couch
and frown.

I open my mouth to speak,
but stop;
my eyes falling
on the framed photo
of Dalisay, Dad and me
on the coffee table.

I think of baked beans,
take a few deep breaths,
wipe the frown off my face
and turn towards Mum.

'Sure Mum, I can do that,' I say,

'no problem.'

That's when good neighbours become good friends.

Dad must've been nervous
on his way up here;
walking past all those suspected "dope dealers"
and "dead beats".

It's his first visit
to our new home
and I can tell
he's feeling uncomfortable.
I can sense it.

I sense it
when he steps through
the front door
 sporting a new beard;
his forehead covered
in sweat.

I sense it
when he sees Mum
standing there,
dressed in her best red skirt,
lipstick on.

I sense it
when Dad shakes my hand
but avoids my eyes.

I sense it
when Mum says,
'Dalisay's not at home,
she's in Mildura,
but she's sent you this letter.'

I sense it
when Dad shoves Dalisay's letter
deep inside his coat pocket,
where it sits unopened,
all night,
like an angry red blister
waiting to pop.

And I sense it
when Dad realises
Mum's gone to the effort
of cooking a bloody roast.

Twenty minutes after his arrival,
 Mum dishes up our meals
and we begin to eat.

I sit at the table
pulling at the too-tough meat on my fork
like a heroin addict
tugging at a tourniquet
before a fix;
frantic for escape.

Pressed in tight,
around our
little round dining table,
Mum, Dad, and me
all sit there
—a taut little human noose
of memory, stress and broken dreams.

There's little conversation
and the slow flow of words
circulating between us
remains shallow.
We chew and swallow
the food on our plates.

I unbutton my shirt's top button
as Dad pours himself a wine
when, all of a sudden,
there's a knock at the door.

Without hesitation
I jump out of my seat,
and rush towards
the welcome sound.

Opening the door,
I peer out into the corridor.

Standing on the other side of the flyscreen
is Johnny Lazzaro,
smiling.

'How ya going brother?' he says,
'Thought I'd drop by.'

I don't respond to Johnny's greeting.

Instead,
I turn towards the dining table,
'Sorry Mum, I'm out of here.'

Before Mum can react
I step out the front door
and drag Johnny,
in a rush of movement,
down the neon-lit vein of corridor outside our flat
and into the stairwell.

In the stairwell
Johnny looks me up and down
and laughs,
'So you're not inviting me in then?' he says.

'Not tonight Johnny,' I say,
undoing another button on my shirt,
'you got somewhere we could go?'

Johnny's place

As we climb
the steps of the stairwell,
floor by floor,
my footsteps get heavy
and my breath shortens.

'Where are you taking me Johnny?'
Don't you live downstairs?'
I ask, turning my head in his direction.

'Brother, you'll see,' Johnny replies,
quickening his pace.

I struggle to keep up
as the big red numbers
painted on the stairwell doors
quickly roll past:

19...
   20...
     21...
       22...

Then, with my legs on the verge of collapsing,
we finally come to a stop
in front of a large white door
with a sign on it:
ROOFTOP EXIT
ACCESS PROHIBITED!

Looped around the door's handle
is a big metal chain
and a large steel padlock.

'So where to now?'
I ask Johnny, looking around bemused.

Johnny ignores my question,
pulling a jangle of keys
from his coat pocket.

He selects a small brassy one,
winks in my direction
and moments later
we're stepping out
onto the tar-coated roof of our apartment block;
suddenly aware
of the sounds of traffic below
and the smell of diesel fumes.

I watch Johnny as he moves over
to one of the ventilation shafts
and waves me over.
'Gimme a hand will ya,' he says.
'Grab the other side of this.'

'Where did you get that key from?' I ask
as Johnny grabs one end
of a large aluminium grill
and I grab the other.
We lift the grill from its housing
and place it on the ground.

'Mate, would you believe me
if I told ya I found it in the lock?'

Johnny reaches into the large cavity behind the grill
and removes an assortment
of second-hand objects.

Johnny folds open a wonky deck chair,
flicks out a weather-beaten rug,
plugs an old stereo into a maintenance power point on
the wall and invites me to sit down.

On the rug,
Johnny places some Rolling Stone magazines,
copies of The Age
and Green Left Weekly,
a pair of binoculars
and a couple of six packs of lukewarm beer.

Grabbing one of the VB stubbies
and throwing it onto my lap,

Johnny speaks.
'I got three rules Pedro,
so ya better listen up.
One, if you drink the beer, put it back.
Two, clean up when you leave.
And three,
this is my place
so don't go stuffing it up.'

Six beers in

I pull myself up in the deck chair
and swallow hard.
'Sit back down you crazy bastard!'
I shout.

But there's no reply.

Johnny stands barefoot,
with his back to me
arm's outstretched,
barely five metres away;
teetering on the rooftop's ledge.

My palms grow wet with sweat as
he slowly lowers his gaze
from the sky above
to the world below.
His profile
—like a scarecrow erected
amongst a field of smog and stars—
stands on guard,
holding back the night.

Me and Johnny.
Six beers in.

'Johnny, are you listening to me?
You're really starting to freak me out!'

Johnny slowly removes his singlet
and throws it over his shoulder,
returning his arms to their outstretched position.

I can almost sense his pleasure
as a little gust of wind
blows across the rooftop,
licking his naked chest.

'Yeah, Pedro, I hear you
but do you hear me?'

'Of course I do you idiot!' I reply.

'Then fucking come over here and take a look.
It's great.
The whole fucked up world at your feet.
It makes you feel alive, Pedro,
it makes you "be" alive!
You wanna "be" alive don't ya?'

'No, I'd prefer to "stay" alive, Johnny,
so stop dicking around
and come back here.'

With my last words
Johnny spins around
and stares at me
before speaking.
'Brother,
you've got some big arse problems.'
He walks back over,
collapses on the rug,
and stares up at the night sky.
'You're living a lie mate.'

'What the hell are you talking about?
What's this "living a lie" crap?'
I snap
'If you think I'm living a lie
then you're deluded.
From my point of view,
you're the one with problems.
Standing on the ledge like that,
half pissed,
well that's bloody crazy;
it's suicide.'

'Well maybe suicide's ok,' Johnny fires back,
'at least it's real.'

I look at Johnny in shock
and our eyes lock.
But as we look at each other
I start to feel like a rabbit;
a rabbit on a lonely road somewhere,
trapped in front of the oncoming blaze

of Johnny's headlight stare.
We look at each other
transfixed
until Johnny finally looks away and laughs,
slapping me on the leg

'Shit, this is hard to explain,
but I'll give it a go,'
he says in a softer voice.
'When I'm standing on the edge,
everything turns upside down.
It's the fucking world, not me,
that's killing itself, brother
—I call it suicide in slow motion.'

'That's bullshit!
That's the biggest load of crap I've ever heard
and you know it!
God, you're such a dickhead.'

'It ain't bullshit, just think 'bout it,
every day people live their lives
saying the same thing that you did before.
They say they'd rather "stay" alive,
than "be" alive.
Now that's what I call bullshit.'

'Well if you're so alive and brave
why don't you just jump?
I'll tell you why;
it's because you're full of shit!
I'm getting tired of this conversation.'

Johnny cracks a huge smile and laughs,
'Brother, don't get so uptight.
I don't jump 'cause I got
reasons for living. Do you?
There's my Dad, my country
and the pain of my people.
I got memories too.
Back in East Timor we didn't have much,
but we were alive;
alive in ways you'd never understand.

What have you got Pedro?
Hey? What have you got?'

Johnny's question sits
like a heavy lead lump
in my guts.
What have I got?
What have I got?

I look down at Johnny
staring up at the sky, smiling
and I think to myself,
'Well apart from Mum and Dal,
perhaps I got you Johnny,
you mad bastard.
Maybe I've got you.'

In the morning

The sun's first rays
paint orange blotches
across the back of my closed eyelids;
my dreaming.
My cocooned eyes
sleep
crust
crack open
like egg shells.
I yawn and stretch.
A new day.

In foetal bliss,
the peaceful shape of Johnny
lies curled up
on the rug beside me.
Johnny sleeps like a dormant power line
pulsing static hum.
The gravelly rhythm of his breathing
buzzes
with latent electrified life.

A new born day.
A rooftop womb.

With Johnny asleep
I stand up
and step over quietly
to the rooftop's ledge.

The morning sun is warm.

I look behind,
double check Johnny's sleeping,
then step out towards the edge
and open my hands wide to the waking world.

"Being" not "staying" alive.
22 storeys high.

The sun
is a broken yolk
drip-drizzled and poured
over the horizon.
Its sticky golden goo covers everything:
the tree tops,
concrete,
glass,
steel,
and the promise of a new day.

I'm rising and dining
on this morning glory,
served up a breakfast
of sizzling delight

Chapter 3:

Cracks in the pavement

Age 17
Richmond

West Heidelberg High

The public transport trip
from Richmond
to West Heidelberg High school
takes almost an hour,
give or take a cancellation or two.
But Mum reckons the time and inconvenience
is a small price to pay
for keeping a little continuity in my life.

It's the first day of year eleven
and as usual
our Principal, Mr Gunther,
stands in front of the school hall
directing traffic.
His booming voice
herds students like flocks of sheep
towards their designated areas
to collect their timetables
and instructions for the day ahead.

Falling in with the crowd,
I follow Miriam Hussein
our Captain,
with her green silk hijab,
down the dimly lit
K-block corridor.
Students stake their claims
to lockers as they go
then pile into the big drama room at K2
where Mr Jefferies walks around
handing out folded pieces of paper
to each new arriving student.
Within minutes I'm nervously holding
the slip of paper
that will reveal my fate.

Around the drama room
sighs of relief,
the odd swear word or two,

moans
and claps of joy
mix together
into one big blob of sound.

A semicircle of unhappy students
surrounds Mr Jefferies,
shaking their slips of paper
in his face
and calling out to him
like traders on the floor
of the wall street stock exchange.

Turning away from the commotion,
I slowly unfold the slip of paper
in my hand,
take a deep breath,
and scan the page below.

The wind goes limp in my sail.

The list reads
like the death notices section
of the local newspaper
—each line heavy
with meaning and misery.

Chemistry	Mrs Haloumi (the Nazi!)
General Maths	Mr Stiller (the dinosaur!)
English	Mr Swaggert
English Literature	Mr Swaggert
History	Mr Swaggert

Marty Brown looks over my shoulder,
takes one look at my list and laughs.
'Shit Pedro, you've got Swaggert the Faggot
for three different classes.
Good luck with that!'
But before I can mount a response
the school bell sounds.

Students start to spill out the door
and I'm pushed along

with the rising torrent of bodies;
swept down corridors
now flooded with noise and commotion.
I pitch and lurch
in search
of my locker,
as wave after wave
 of students
push, crash
and shove their way past me.
Caught
in a whitewash of
new school uniforms,
a final wave of students
 peaks and breaks past me for class.

Finally, the buffeting subsides
and I find myself standing in front of my locker
—rudderless, a capsized boat.

I quickly tuck my shirt in,
grab my books
and run as fast as I can to
my first class.

History
with Mr Swaggert.

Lessons in History

Mr Swaggert stands
at the entrance of the portable
greeting each student
as they enter.

As I pass
he shakes my hand
and whispers in my ear:
'Don't think
you can slack off
like last year, Pedro.
I'm expecting big things from you.'

Fifteen minutes later
and the class is in full swing.
Mr Swaggert is his normal self,
waltzing around the room
in his double-breasted suit,
neatly ironed white shirt
and silk tie.
After his standard introduction
he writes the heading,
AUSTRALIAN HISTORY on the board
in big, beautiful
cursive letters
and asks us to pay attention.

'All right guys,
here's the deal.
Australian history is a great subject
so let's hit the ground running.
I want to see what you're made of.'

A classroom
of blank expressions
and vacant holiday eyes
stares back in Swaggert's direction.

'We're going to start things off
with a research assignment.

What I want you to do
is investigate a major historical event
that has helped to shape Australia
in a positive way
and given us a real sense
of national pride and identity.
This is a fantastic assignment guys
and it will deepen your appreciation
of our great land.'

Mr Swaggert walks around
and hands us an assignment sheet.

'You'll notice that I've included
a few suggestions,
just in case you get stuck.
Topics like Gallipoli
and the ANZAC legend,
or our famous
America's Cup victory in the eighties
would be perfect,
 but please,
 feel free to come up with your own ideas
—surprise me!'

Looking down at the assignment sheet,
I read the instructions
and scratch my head.

'Oh, and by the way,' Mr Swaggert interrupts,
'assessment will be based on a speech
to be delivered
in front of class
in four weeks time.'

The classroom lets out
a collective groan
as the reality of a new school year
suddenly sets in.

Lessons in English

It's the end of day one
and school concludes
with Mr Swaggert
in the Drama room,
a double period of English
and the "brave new world" of William Shakespeare.

After a few words
about Western literature,
Swaggert says
that in order to study
our first play, *Macbeth*
we need to get our heads
around some of Shakespeare's sonnets.

Then the gibberish
really begins.

Swaggert introduces us to concepts
like "rhyming schemes", "metaphors"
and "clichés".
He goes on to explain
how Shakespeare
liked to write in 'iambic pentameter'
which roughly translated
means 'the rhythm of five heartbeats.'

'Listen carefully
and you'll hear
the melodic and transcendent qualities
of the rhythm,' he says,
holding up his hand to his ear
before reciting another line of poetry.

What a tosser!

To illustrate his point further,
Swaggert gets us to stand up
and walk around
in a big circle;

stamping our feet in time
to a soft/hard,
da/DUM,
da/DUM,
da/DUM rhythm.
He then tells us to repeat
after him
the lines of Shakespeare's 18th sonnet
as we march:

'Shall **I** com**pare** thee **to a summer**'s **day**?
Thou **art** more **lovely and** more **temperate**:
Rough **winds** do **shake** the **darling buds** of **May**.
And **summer**'s **lease** hath **all** too **short** a **date**'.

All around me
students giggle,
blush,
moan
and play the fool.
On the opposite side of the circle
Marco Lombardi river dances
while Sam McKenzie does a rap version of each line.

'To understand Shakespeare,
you have to understand how the language works,'
Swaggert yells out as we stamp our feet,
'and to understand how it works
you have to live it and experience it!'

All of a sudden
Marco Lombardi falls to the ground,
taking three other students with him.

Laughter breaks out
in all directions.

Swaggert blows his top.

'Right, if you're going to muck up
we'll do things the hard way.
For homework tonight,
I expect each and every one of you

to write a
Shakespearean sonnet.
—no excuses!'

And then,
just when I thought
things couldn't get any worse,
Swaggert orders me
(and me alone!)
to stand in front of the entire class
and demonstrate how 'a good student'
(like myself!)
is able to complete
an easy exercise like this
with a minimum of fuss.

In front of twenty-two
thank-God-it's-not-me faces,
I reluctantly repeat Swaggert's lines
as my feet da/Dum da/Dum,
up and down,
through invisible
      ankle deep
mud.

'Rough **winds** do **shake** the **darling buds** of **May**.
And **summer's lease** hath **all** too **short** a **date**'.

Rooftop Homework

I take out the key
Johnny had cut for me
and slip it into the lock.

A few seconds later,
I'm standing on the roof
of Eden Towers
in my own
private
sky rise study.
I fold out
the old banana lounge
I'd scavenged from the Salvos
the week before
and sit down.

Opening my school bag,
I pull out my English workbook
and turn to a fresh page.
I write the heading,
"A Sonnet for Swaggert"
up the top.

Chewing on the end
of my HB pencil,
I picture Swaggert strutting around in class
like a B-grade game show host,
and wait in hope
for some inspiration
to arrive.

My poem: "A Sonnet for Swaggert"

Shall **I** compare you **to** a **Shake**speare **play**?
You **are** more **wordy and** more **second rate**:
Rough **kids** do **push** you **round** the **class** all **day**,
And **write** on **desks** that **you're** the **one** they **hate**:
Some**times** too **hot** the **eye** of **heaven shines**,
And **in** your **class** we **swelter** in the **heat**;
and **every word** you **speak** into our **minds**,
soon **dies** from **thirst**, or **smells** like **rotted meat**;
But **blind** you **soldier on** and **do** not **fade**
Nor **lose** possession **of** that **smile** you **give**;
You'll **stay** forever **as** a **tired** cliché
'cause **in** these **lines** of **mine** you'll **always live**;
So **long** as **kids** can **breathe**, and **word** can **spread**,
We'll **join** your **class** weighed **down** with **fear** and **dread**.

Pretty good with words

'What ya got there, brother,' Johnny says,
placing his guitar case on the ground
and flopping down beside me.

'It's my English homework. I have to...'
but before I can finish my sentence,
Johnny leans over
and grabs the workbook off my lap.

'Come on Johnny,
give it back!' I yell,
reaching out.

But Johnny turns his back on me,
coiling himself around my workbook.
A moment later,
in a loud, sinister voice
he hisses out the words to my poem,
instantly picking up on the mood.

I lie back down on the lounge,
defeated,
and listen to
the venomous words of my sonnet
as they slither off Johnny's tongue.

The rhythm of five poisoned heartbeats.

'Shit man, you're pretty good with words,' Johnny says,
looking up from the page
and turning in my direction.
'But if you wanna know what I reckon,
I think you need to move on.
If you hate school so much,
why don't you just fucking leave?'

'Geez Johnny, it's not that easy.
And anyway, if I left school,
what would I do?
Absolutely nothing like you?'

An instant pang of regret
fills my gut
as my flippant words hit their mark.
 Johnny's smile
crumples to a frown.

'Mate, you've got no idea, have ya?
Don't you ever listen to me?
I told you, I'm an asylum seeker;
an asylum seeker for fucking God's sake!
Look at me, brother, I got no future here
—can't work,
even if I wanted to.
It's against the law.
I haven't got any choice in the matter,
you stupid prick.
Why else do you reckon I busk?'

'Sorry Johnny,
I didn't mean to say that.
I'm really sorry.'

'Yes you did, Pedro.
Fuck mate, don't bullshit me.
You ain't sorry,
just fucking wrong!
I work harder than you think.
I do heaps of things.
If you stepped outside
that bubble you're living in
maybe you'd see that.'

Johnny throws my workbook on the ground
and turns in the other direction.
He pulls out his guitar
from its case,
and with angry fingers,
starts giving the instrument
a well needed tune.

I sit there
thinking about the truth
in Johnny's words.

Swallowing my pride,
I speak up.

'You're right Johnny,
I haven't been listening.
I'm sorry.
That's no way
to treat a friend.'

The guitar strings stop their twanging
as Johnny turns to face me.

'Well don't tell me, show me, Pedro.
If you're really sorry,
and you're really my mate,
then you better come out with me
to one of me Sanctuary Network gigs.
It's time you got
a real education.'

'Sure, Johnny, whatever you want,'
I say without hesitation.

Johnny smiles,
    deep and sharp,
'Well, come to think of it,
there is something else,' he says.

'What's that?' I ask.

Johnny chops down
on the strings of his guitar.
A big thunderous chord,
as dark as a storm cloud,
rumbles through the air.
'It's time you learnt how to busk, Pedro.
Yep, you heard me! It's time you learnt how to busk.'

Lessons in Busking

With a fine silky mist
hanging in the air,
Johnny plays guitar
and teaches me the lyrics
to some of his favourite songs.

Bob Marley,
Dylan,
Midnight Oil,
Nirvana.

Johnny demonstrates the finer points
of singing in harmony
and after a little practise
I marvel
at the way our voices
climb and twist
around each other
like a tangle of vines.

Johnny says I've got a good voice.

Handing me
an old pair of drumsticks
from his backpack,
Johnny then gets me to tap along
to the music.
It's hard to coordinate,
but my hands slowly
find the tempo;
beating out a rattle-tap-tap
on the back of Johnny's
empty guitar case.

Johnny says I've got a good sense of rhythm too.

For the next hour
we work on a set of songs
that Johnny says
are good for busking.

Then Johnny plays one more song,
but this time
he sings it all alone.

'This is one of me favourite songs,'
Johnny says before starting.
'It sums up what I stand for, Pedro,
like no other song.
But I don't want you getting
the wrong fucking idea.
It's not a religious song.'

God bless the grass (lyrics in Appendix)

(Clearly influenced
by voices on the radio,
Johnny sings
with a slight American accent
and I find it a little amusing.

But as Johnny sings
"God Bless the Grass"
I quickly forget
about the accent.
Underneath, Johnny's voice is clean
and pure and as I listen
something in me changes forever.

The vibe of the song
sends a shiver
up my spine,
while the words
plant a seed
deep within
my dirt poor heart.)

When words take flight

When Johnny leaves
I rip the sonnet from my workbook,
fold it into the shape
of a paper plane
and launch it from the rooftop.

The plane drifts across the sky
then spiral-falls
towards the ground below.

It falls
from the weight of the words
it carries.

It falls,
speeding towards
 the cracks in the pavement
below.

It falls,
dragging my anger
behind it.

Tunnel busking

Saturday morning,
Friday night
and sometimes after school.
(Johnny and me,
the kings of busking!)

We wander the CBD
and the congested streets of Richmond
in search of loose change
and receptive audiences.

We busk
outside train stations,
entertaining the peak hour crowds.

We busk
outside Gate 7 of the MCG
as footy supporters
descend in packs;

and we busk
outside pubs
waiting for the drunks inside
to stumble home,
throwing coins.

But our favourite place to busk
is down in the tunnels
under Melbourne.

Deep underground,
in the tunnels of the city loop,
'the acoustics sound sweet!'

Deep underground
the tap of my drumsticks on a metal can
        rattles like gunfire.

Deep underground
Johnny's voice
echoes like a mountain wind.

And deep underground
Johnny and me
can make good money
—almost twenty bucks an hour
from the coin-jangled pockets
of those passing by.

Turning Japanese?

At the end of each busking session
Johnny gives me a nod
and we break into our final song.

It's always the same tune
and we perform it
as a duet,
taking it in turns to sing
each line.

As we sing,
our laughter always threatens to ruin
our performance:

'Turning Japanese.'

'I think I'm turning Japanese.'

'I really think so.'

'Turning Japanese.'

'I think I'm turning Japanese.'

'I really think so.'

Johnny and me think it's the funniest thing.

A half-Filipino student

and an East Timorese asylum seeker

    turning Japanese

with a bunch of beady-eyed customers looking on,

        unable to spot the difference.

The Riser

The Rising Sun Hotel
on Swan Street,
or "The Riser",
as locals like to call it,
is Johnny's favourite pub.

Down at The Riser
beer-drenched bar towels
squelch
then drip
amber fluid
onto never-polished floorboards.

Down at The Riser
the wallpaper is stained brown
by time
and the memory of smoke
from a thousand
tar-stained fingers.

Down at The Riser
bulbous-nosed, old men
drink beer
and mind their own business;
shifting their focus
from their form guides
to the tote,
then back again
to the bar
in one long endless cycle.

And down at The Riser
there's a "free-to-play"
pool table,
Richmond's cheapest beer
and a publican
who never asks questions.

Last drinks?

On Saturday,
the 24th of February,
Johnny introduces me to my first "big session"
of drinking
after receiving a letter from his father
in prison.

Johnny tells me nothing
    about the letter's contents.

Johnny just needs a friend.

So for three long hours
Johnny and me
slurp down pots of Carlton,
    slap pool balls into pockets
and stumble off
to the toilets
where we sway in front
of the urinal
—dissolving yellow cakes of disinfectant
with our piss.

By the time the barman calls for last drinks,
my world is spinning out of control.

My pool cue
divots
the table,
    my glass of beer
breaks on the floor
         and I stagger back
to the toilets,
my stomach now fighting
       a war.

Discovering my need for God

A toilet cubical

   Kneeling in submission

On the phone to God

   A brown-flecked
porcelain receiver

I vomit
and cry out:

'God, make it stop!
Please, I'll never drink again!'

The world spins around
   and around
      and around.
But it's not God who answers.

It's Johnny.

It's Johnny who helps me to stand,

Johnny who cleans me up

   and Johnny who guides me home

—my arm

   draped over his shoulder.

When cracks first appear

Feelings of vertigo,

Sunday morning.

My hung-over head
              throbbing
   with the imaginary sound
of a thousand angry cicadas.

Hitching up my pyjamas,
I walk into the lounge room
and I stand in front of Mum
ready to speak.

'Why aren't you dressed for Mass, Pedro?'
Mum asks, 'I called out to you
a long time ago.'

Mum's question hangs in the air
like bathroom mist.
My palms turn
wet and sticky
as I stand there,
suddenly lost for words.

Mum sits
at the table
   with a steamy cup
of green tea in her hands,
dressed up
in her
best
Sunday
outfit.

I take a deep breath,
scratch my chin
and boldly open my mouth to speak.
But the words come out
in a trickle;

like water
from a
leaky
tap.

'Mum,
I'm not going
to Mass anymore.'

Mum's reaction is immediate.

'What are you saying, Pedro?
You made me a promise.
If you break your word,
you'll break my heart.'

Time suddenly slows to a tiptoe.

The clock on the wall
hides its face.

And I sit down at the table,
pushed down
by an unbearable weight.

When cracks first appear II

'Mum, if I could go to Mass,
I would,
but I can't anymore;
I can't live a lie.'

Mum turns away
in frustration
and reaches
for the packet of Longbeach
on the table.
She puts a cigarette
in her mouth
and lights up.

A silence
heavier than memory
descends on the space
between us;
blanketing us
in our own private thoughts.

When I finally find the will
to speak,
my previously slow,
careful selection of words is gone,
replaced by a rushing stream of sentences.

'Mum, I don't want to hurt you,
but I've really had enough
of the whole religious thing.
You can't make me go to Mass anymore.
I'm an adult now.
And anyway, how can you expect me
to go to church
when I'm not even sure
I believe in God.
I'm not like you;
I don't have your faith.'

Mum taps her ash into the teacup.

'Mum, are you listening to me?
You can't make me believe in God
and you can't keep telling me
that the Catholic Church
has all the answers!'

Mum reaches for a second cigarette.

'You gotta stop being
so worried about me.
I can't hack it anymore.
I need to find
my own way in life.'

Mum sits there
unwilling
or simply
too angry
to respond;
the smell
of disappointment
in the air
more pungent
than the smoke.

Faced with a no win situation,
my words slip quickly
        into open revolt.

'It's bullshit, Mum!
Can't you see it?
Johnny does!
If God really exists
then why is there so much crap
in our world?
Shit, Mum, if God is love,
why doesn't he do something?
It doesn't make sense, Mum.
It doesn't add up.'

Mum stamps her butt
into the teacup
and stands up.

'I'm late,' she says,
picking up her handbag
and walking towards the door.

The front door spins on its hinges,
slamming violently shut.
The force of the impact
dislodging Mum's favourite
leather bound Bible
from the bookshelf.

Feathers for pages,
the bible drops,
flapping
like a wounded bird
to the floor.

Mum tells me

When Mum finally talks to me again
                 it's from the end of my bed
      late on Sunday night.

She sits on my doona,
with her legs crossed.
Her voice is measured
and surprisingly calm
as she starts to speak.

'You upset me
very much,' she says.
'You were very rude
to me,' she says.
'I'm not as stupid
as you say,' she says.

To prove her point,
Mum removes a piece of paper
from her pocket.
The crumpled page is covered
in Mum's distinctive
handwriting.
On one side
is a heavy Spanish scrawl:
on the other side,
a hasty looking English translation.

'I thought all day
about what you say to me Pedro,
then I write this letter,' Mum says.

Before reading the letter out,
Mum says,
'Pedro, I think you were right.
I can't make you believe
in God.
But I am your mother
and this is my flat.
So if you want to stop going to Mass

you will have to give me
something in return.
After that, I will leave you alone,'
she says, 'After that,
you can work it out
for yourself.'

Pissed off

Mum reads me
her letter
and some of it
actually makes sense.

But some of it
just pisses me off.

In particular,
Mum preaches some rubbish
to me about
"what faith is"
and "why it's good".

She also tells me
that I'm wrong
about God.

'Pedro, faith in God
is not the important thing.
The important thing
is that God has faith in you.
God needs you,
Pedro,
just like I need you.
You say God does nothing,
but maybe that's because
God is waiting for you
to give him a hand.
Maybe God needs you, Pedro.
Maybe God needs you.'

A small request?

Smart,
sly,
shrewd,
scheming words.

With her preaching at an end,
Mum moves on
to explain
her one "small request".

Mum says
she'd like me to help Evie,
the little girl
from down the hall,
set up a garden.

Mum says
that Evie came
down to the community garden
the other day
and that she was so excited
that she
signed Evie up
for her own plot.
'But Evie is just little, Pedro,
and her Mother is not well enough
to help.
But, if you help Evie make her garden,
I'll never ask you
to go to Mass again.'

Mum's scheming words
roll off the tip of her tongue
like loaded dice.

Her request tumbles up the doona
and lands with a rattle
inside my head.

From the end of the bed
Mum gives me a knowing smile
—a smile clearly slanted in her favour —
and waits patiently
for my reply.

Staked to the ground

I place Miss January
back into her hiding place under my desk
and slide the bottom drawer
back into place.

It's half past midnight.
and as I get back into bed
I start thinking about
my new agreement with Mum,
my hatred for gardening
and the hard-staked roses
I used to look after
at Grandma Jones' house.

Free from the Catholic Mass;
I moan at the thought of myself
now staked to the ground
of the community garden
like one of those imprisoned roses.

It's a sad saying
that roses
    always hide their thorns.

But it's true.

I bury my face into the pillow.

    Sleep swallows up the night.

After two months of busking

After two months of busking,
the old Milo tin
with its glued down lid
and coin slit,
is three quarters full with coins.

'There must be two hundred bucks
in there, brother,' Johnny says to me one day,
lifting the tin off the desk.

Sometimes,
late at night,
I sit at my desk alone,
pick up the heavy green tin
and feel the weight
of possibilities it contains.

But more often than not,
I hold up
the makeshift moneybox
and simply smile
at the fact
that it isn't the coins
making the tin so goddamned heavy,
it's the wealth of happy memories
accumulated within
that give it so much weight.

Dear Dad

Inspired by Dalisay
I write my own letter to Dad
and place it in a plain white envelope.

Dear Dad,

Don't listen to Mum. She might say I need you, but I don't miss you one bit and I'm better off without you. You might as well go on living your life as if you had no kids, because the truth is, I don't want you as a Father anymore. If sons could divorce their Fathers then I reckon life would be a bit easier for both of us. Anyway, I haven't got much else to say. I've included some tickets to Luna Park. In case you didn't know, I won them last year at school. They expire next week and I don't need them. There's something I don't like about that clown's face anyway, you know, the one guarding the entrance. I think it reminds me a bit too much of you.

Your mail order son,

Pedro Adam Jones.

Inside the envelope,
along with the letter
and the family pass to Luna Park,
I place a poem that I'd found
while surfing the Internet at school.

I seal the envelope
with a lick
and scribble Dad's address
on to the front.
On the back I write
my name and address as:

Pedro Ongpauco
Out of sight,
out of mind.

The poem: 'Roller Coaster'

Who needs a ticket
to a Luna Park
when the roller coaster bar
fastens down over our heads
with a dry mechanical click
every day
round here.

Our carriages move
then grind and squeal
to a jolt
forward
as we're hauled again
up the track
with screams
before the fall.

Clickity clack,
clickity clack,
never look back
you should never look back.

Round here we leave our hands in the carriage
close our eyes
and hold on.
Our fingers grip tight
to knuckle white
the steel rod
across our knees;
offering coldness
and only the illusion of safety.

Clickity clack,
clickity clack,
never look back
you should never look back.

Eyes straight ahead
help avoid the signs
of track disrepair:

the flaking paint,
rusted bolts
and dry rot.
Is there anyone doing the maintenance
around here anyway?

Clickity clack,
over the skeleton's back
clickity clack
waiting for these wooden ribs to snap
with a clickity crack
clickity crack.

Up and down,
faster and faster,
we ride until it hurts,
over and over again,
day after day.

We rise then fall,
with the wind whip-beating our eyes
to a wet
shimmer shimmer gleam.

The rotary club gig

Johnny throws his guitar case
into the back of the minibus
and tells me to get in.

Sliding the side door open,
I step inside the van
and sit down
next to an old man
wearing a sweat-stained akubra hat.

The old man's deep facial lines,
flaky white skin
and whiskered nose
point to
an age somewhere past seventy.

'G'day mate, I'm Paddy,' the old man says,
extending his hand
in my direction.

'Hi, I'm...'
but before I can finish my greeting,
Johnny plonks himself down
in the seat in front of me
and turns around
to speak.

'Hey everyone,
meet Pedro.
He's my mate
and he's here to check us out
and see what we do.'
Johnny cracks a smile
and gives me a wink
before continuing.
'He's busting
to join our group,
so make him feel at home.'

I give Johnny
a long, dirty look
as a bunch of warm greetings
reach me
from all corners
of the minibus.

Johnny then introduces me individually
to everyone on board.

'The legend you're sitting next to
is Paddy O'Leary, Pedro.
Fernando Gutteres is the ugly looking Timorese bloke
with the hairy mop of hair
in the driver's seat.
And that's Sister McKenzie,
one of the group's founders
by his side.
The sexy-looking babe
up the back
is Lisa McCosh
and that's Brendan Piper,
our Chairman,
on her left.'

The young woman
sitting up the back,
with the shaven head
and green tank top,
looks up angrily at Johnny.

'Johnny, you know I hate it
when you say derogatory things
like that,' she says.

'Yeah,
I know Lisa.
Like always, I'm sorry.'

Lisa looks past Johnny
towards the front of the bus
and raises her voice,
'Hey Fernando, looks like Johnny's

in one of those annoying moods again.
You better turn up the radio
just in case he gets on a roll.'

Johnny gives a chuckle,
'Ok boss,
I'll shut me mouth then.'

'You better Johnny,' Fernando says,
swinging around in the front seat,
'The Hawthorn Rotary Club
are interested in supporting us.
I don't want you to stuff up our chances.
I want tonight to go
as smoothly as possible.'

Fernando starts up the motor
and pulls out from the kerb
with a jolt.

For the next twenty minutes,
I sit in my seat
and chat to Paddy O'Leary while Johnny
stares quietly out the window,
clearly embarrassed by his actions.

By the time we reach our destination
Johnny hasn't made a peep
and I make a mental note
of the fact
that tonight is the first time
I've ever seen Johnny
completely lost for words.

The rotary club gig II

Standing out the front
of the East Hawthorn Council Rooms,
Johnny puts his guitar case down
and opens up
his packet of Drum.
'Grab a seat inside, Pedro.
I'll be in later,' he says,
dropping a lump of tobacco into his palm
and licking the edge of his Tally-Ho.

With his eyes staring up
at the empty flagpole on the lawn,
I can tell Johnny
wants to be left alone.

Paddy taps me on the back
and ushers me over
to the front door of the hall.
'Don't wait up for Johnny, mate.
He never comes in
until after the film's been shown.'

Paddy and me make our way
through the front door
and into the gathering space within.

Inside,
the aroma
of freshly brewed tea
wafts over us
from a table
laden with biscuits and cakes
 to the side.

Surveying the room,
I manage to count the presence
of twenty-two people,
before a smiling,
bespectacled old lady
steps out in front of me,

grinning from ear to ear.
'I'm Wilma,' she says,
shaking my hand
and guiding me over
to the 'good seats'
at the front of the hall.

'It's an honour to have so many
East Timorese people
with us tonight.
We're so happy
you could make it,' she says.
'Now, could I get you anything to drink?
A cup of tea perhaps?'

'No thanks,' I answer,
smiling politely,
'and by the way,
I'm not East Timorese,
I'm Australian.'

Wilma's cheeks turn redder
than her nail polish.
'Well of course you're Australian,'
        she says awkwardly
before scurrying off
to help the others find their seats.

Paddy turns to me
and gives a little laugh,
'Shit mate, don't scare them off
too quick.
At the rate you're going,
I'll end up giving my speech
to an audience of one!'

The Sanctuary Network

Grabbing the microphone
and adjusting her cardigan,
Sister McKenzie
gives a brief opening speech
about the history of East Timor.

Sister McKenzie
describes how in 1975,
the newly independent nation of East Timor
was brutally invaded
by Indonesian armed forces.

Sister McKenzie speaks professionally,
but without much spark,
and her lack of charisma is so noticeable
that I start to feel guilty
about not fully engaging
with her speech.

Turning my gaze
towards the front entrance of the hall,
I catch a glimpse of Johnny through the window
as he lights up another rollie.
The sight of Johnny
reminds me
that I need to pay better attention.
After all, Johnny wanted me
to find out
who he was
and what made him tick.
And as his friend,
I needed
to follow through on my promise.

With Sister McKenzie's lifeless voice
hanging in the air,
I straighten myself up
and try to refocus
on what's being said.

'The Sanctuary Network
is made up of a everyday Australians
who have pledged to illegally harbour and hide
East Timorese asylum seekers
who are threatened with deportation
by our government.
This is a courageous commitment.
Our members are agreeing
to potentially break the law
and go to jail
in order to protect
the 1500 asylum seekers
who arrived on our shores
after the Dili Massacre in 1991...'

Using a lot of facts and figures,
Sister McKenzie continues to speak to us
for another ten minutes
on the subject
before inviting
the old time wharfie and digger,
Paddy O'Leary,
to get up
and deliver a few words
on the issue.

Feeling overwhelmed
by Sister McKenzie's fancy language,
I still manage to get the general gist
of what's been said.
In particular, I manage to work out three things.

One,
my refugee mate, Johnny
isn't welcome in Australia
and might be thrown out of the country
at any moment.

Two,
there's a bunch
of decent Australians out there,
from all walks of life,

willing to go to jail
because they're pissed off
with our government's heartless stance
on the matter.

And three,
Johnny had fled East Timor because of something
horrific   called the Dili Massacre
and as his best mate, I hadn't even bothered
to find out what that was.

Five rounds with Paddy,

A grizzly old prize fighter,
Paddy steps up
to the front of the stage
like he's entering a boxing ring.

Using a combination
of fiery words
and animated gestures,
Paddy punches out
a passionate message that instantly connects
with his audience.
His words are
flung out with gusto:
    swift
           and lethal.

Round 1

Paddy begins
by explaining how he
joined the Australian army
and served in East Timor
during World War II.

'I was working on the East Swanston Dock
when I heard on the radio
that the Japanese Air Force
had just bombed Pearl Harbour.
It was December 7, 1941,' Paddy explains.
'I stood up,
threw down me gear
and walked straight outta there.
The foreman asked me where I was going
and I said I was off to fight a war.'

'Two months later
on January 28, 1942,
I landed in East Timor
with the 2nd Independent Company.
But by that stage of the war,
Australia was in big trouble.
The Japanese had a strangle hold
on most of Asia.
As soon as me and me mates set foot in East Timor
we thought we'd all be dead before year's end,'
Paddy says.
'But thanks to the East Timorese,
most of us lived to tell the tale.
The East Timorese were our only support.
They fed us, guided us through the hills,
carried our gear
and cared for us
when we got sick
with malaria
and dysentery.

The East Timorese,

they were our brothers.'

Round 2

Paddy pauses for a moment
to collect his thoughts,
his bruised memories
 clearly sweeping back through time
to spar with some unseen enemy.
When he comes back to reality,
he quickly wipes away the tears
collecting under his eyes
and continues his attack.

'The East Timorese never betrayed us,' Paddy says.
'The Timorese were loyal to us, like family.
And without their loyalty
us diggers would have been slaughtered up there.
Without their support,
I wouldn't be standing here tonight,
five decades later,
telling you about the debt
me and me mates still owe them people.
It's a debt that has never been repaid.
It's a debt that all Australians have inherited.'

Fernando passes Paddy a glass of water
who gladly takes a long deep sip;
water flicking over the rim. Then,
taking a few breaths to steady himself,
Paddy puts the glass down
and prepares himself
for another round of talking.

Round 3

Paddy's onslaught
doesn't slow down
as his verbal blows
continue to rain down
on the audience:

'One of the hardest things to accept
is that Australia shouldn't have been
in East Timor in the first place.
East Timor was a bloody neutral country back in '42.
They weren't at war.
Yet the East Timorese still bloody helped us,' Paddy says.
'History has forgotten the fact
that 60,000 East Timorese
died for us during the war.
The East Timorese died for us
in battle.
They died for us from torture.
And they died for us from starvation.
Shit, the bloody Japs got so angry with them
they'd burn their villages to the ground
just for suspecting that they'd helped us.
I saw it with me own eyes!
And then, at the end of the war
our government had the nerve
to airdrop a message over East Timor.

And you know what it bloody said?

It said this:

"Your friends will never forget you".'

Round 4

Already reeling from the impact of Paddy's story
and the horrible historical facts,
Paddy then throws out his opinion
like a nasty left hook:

'Australians who turn their backs
on these people
are bloody mugs
and a disgrace to our nation.
Mark my word,
we owe the East Timorese
a historical debt.
Our survival in World War II
was written on the pages of history
in their blood.
They saved our sorry arses
from Japanese invasion
back in '42
and it's about time
we paid them back.'

Glued to our ringside seats,
the only sound I hear
is the occasional movement of hands
removing handkerchiefs and tissues
from pockets and purses.

Round 5

Paddy's voice gets louder
as he starts his final round,
directing a combination of
scathing attacks
at our Government
for not doing enough to prevent
Indonesia from invading East Timor
in 1975:

'Our government is full of
gutless cowards.
For 24 years
those bastards have looked on
while the Indonesian army
has murdered over
a third of the East Timorese population.
That's two hundred thousand people!

Now that's not just a number for God's sake,

    that's me bloody mates!

And don't start me talking about
all the tortures and rapes.
As a nation,
we should feel bloody ashamed!'

But as if Paddy's words weren't already enough,
without any notice,
the knockout punch arrives
    when,
in front of a crowd of 22 onlookers,
Paddy's fighting words
suddenly turn
from anger
to pain
and finally
to open weeping.

Standing in front of us,
the brave old digger's face drains of colour,
his legs start to wobble
and he cries.

He doesn't stop crying.

Rushing to his side,
Brendan catches Paddy under the arm
and eases him down
on to a hastily positioned chair.
Undoing his top button
and removing his Akubra hat,
Brendan quickly calls for
a wet cloth.

Upon arrival
he wipes Paddy's forehead
and wraps the cloth around his neck.

Brendan eases Paddy back into
his front row seat
and after a few minutes
gets up to say Paddy's alright.

Scraping my heart off the canvas,
I wonder if I'll be able to cope with what might follow
or whether I should just
close my eyes,
    shut my ears
                and stay down for the count.

The fight continues

Brendan Piper's words
are smelling salts
and his gaze
a slap on the cheek
that gets your attention,
quick.
Yes, Brendan is the kinda guy
you want in your corner of the ring.
He's the kinda guy
who'd look you in the eye
and tell you to dig deep.
He's the kinda guy you'd fight for;
whose smile alone
could lift your spirits off the canvas
when you're ready to throw in the towel.

And more than that,
Brendan's the kinda guy
who'd tell you the truth
even if it hurt,
take the time to patch up your wounded knowledge
and apply liniment
to your punch-swollen heart.

Standing in front of us,
Brendan takes control of the meeting,
answers all our nagging questions
and checks on Paddy one last time
before explaining to us
the significance of the Dili Massacre.
Brendan tells us
that most of the East Timorese refugees
looking for asylum in Australia
are here as a result
of that one sickening event.

Wheeling out a television and video
to the front of the stage,
Brendan then says he's going to show us

the smuggled out film footage
of the Dili Massacre
that made headlines around the world in 1991.
Brendan says
it's important that we watch it
because it's
an appropriate introduction
for the last presenter
of the night,
Juan Lazzaro,
who fled the massacre in 1991
as a ten-year-old boy.

Before pressing play

With the tape ready to roll,
Brendan stops for a moment
to say a few final words
before pressing play.

'The 5000 East Timorese people
who gathered
at the Santa Cruz Cemetery
in Dili in 1991
had no idea that
271 of them would be killed
and many more wounded.
After this video
Juan Lazzaro
is going to come in here
and sing you a song
about the massacre.'

'Juan's father was shot through the leg
during the massacre
and his mother was shot dead in his arms.
Juan's waiting outside
because this footage is simply
too hard for him to handle.'

'Juan is the real face
of the Sanctuary Network
and the reason that we need your support.'

Another place

Up in front of us,
	guitar in hand,
Johnny stands.
His eyes are on the audience,
but I can tell he's staring right through us.

Johnny's in another place.

Maybe he's still standing
amongst the sounds of gunfire
and the screams
that reached him
from under the hall's front door.

Or perhaps,
in his mind,
he's back in East Timor,
crouched beside his mother's grave.

Wherever he is
I'll never know,
but by the way Johnny sings
I know it's a place of infinite sadness;

	a place of vast

and unfathomable

	grief.

Johnny's song (lyrics in the Appendix)

All that's left

When Johnny finishes his singing,
Brendan slowly gets up
and removes the tape
from the VCR.

Sitting on my chair,
                    speechless,
I try to make sense
of the feelings
burning a path through my body,
but it's too hard.
Nothing solid remains.
Everything is consumed in fire.

I am a burnt out shell
filled only
with the blackened, angry remains
    of my still smouldering heart.

My ignorance lies in ruins.

And all that's left
are my tears,
        my rage
    and my head full of ash.

A topic emerges

The cup of tea goes cold in my hands
as I amble around
the long trestle table
set up by Sister McKenzie
in the corner of the hall.

I examine the vast array of goods on offer.
There's videos,
posters,
pamphlets,
East Timorese scarves,
badges,
stickers,
and books.

Many of the titles on display
look like they belong
to the horror movie section
of a video store:
"Death of a nation",
"A Not-So-Distant Horror",
"Complicity in genocide".

Browsing the titles,
I reach down
and pick up a thin little book
with a shiny red cover.
The title jumps off the binder:

They left us to die:
Australia's hidden history,

And that's when it happens.
At that very moment
a topic for my history assignment
pops into my head
as unexpectedly as a smile from a bouncer.

My head starts filling
    with ideas.

I flick the book over,
read the blurb on the back of the jacket
and realise I've stumbled onto something really powerful;
something that's going to put
Swaggert's head in a spin.

I spend the next half an hour
talking through my new idea
with Lisa,
Sister McKenzie and Brendan,
who all nod their heads in approval
and even extend me offers of help.

By the time I climb back into the minibus
I'm carrying with me
a new sense of purpose;
a show bag full of useful books,
videos
and brochures from Sister McKenzie;
a promise from Paddy and Johnny
to come to my class to speak;
a Sanctuary Network
membership form;
details about the next meeting;
and an appreciative slap on my back from Johnny.

'I'm glad you came tonight, PJ,' Johnny says,
back to his old bubbly self
and pushing me further into the minibus.
'It's good to have you on board.'

Trust Johnny to get it right

'PJ,' I think to myself
as I climb into bed,
remembering what Johnny had called me.
'I reckon I could get used to that.'

Pedro had always been
so goddamned Spanish.

And Jones?
Well Jones had never suited
the colour of my skin.

But PJ
had a cool ring to it.

Dressed up in my new identity,
I snuggle under the doona
and smile.

Sleep swallows up the night.

The proposal

Mr Swaggert's desk
is neater
than his manicured moustache.

Tapping his fingers
on the corners of his arm chair,
he looks up at me.

'So what you're proposing,
if I've got this right,
is that you'd like to bring
a couple of guest speakers into my class
to help you with your presentation
—is that right, Pedro?'

'Yes, Mr Swaggert.'

'Well isn't that a bit excessive Pedro?
There's a time limit
to these speeches, you know.
Why should I allow this?'

I give Swaggert three good reasons why.

First,
I tell him that my speech
is going to be something really special.
'It's all about Australians
and their ability to make sacrifices
throughout history,' I say with enthusiasm.

Second,
I tell him that one of my guest speakers
is an Aussie digger
who fought in World War II.

And third,
I tell him that I've also
enlisted the help
of a "highly gifted musician"
who's willing to perform a song

on my topic
that's simply amazing.

Swaggert becomes putty
in my hands.

'Marvellous, that sounds marvellous, Pedro.
I think the whole class will benefit from this.'

I leave the office
feeling guilty about the half-truths
I'd just spread,
but mindful of their effect:
        leaving
a permanent patriotic smile
plastered across Swaggert's face.

Caught somewhere
between happiness and terror
I contemplate going back
and 'fessing up'
to my real intentions.

 But the thought of
 watching Swaggert,
having to listen to Johnny's song
and then go
five rounds with Paddy,
stops me in my tracks.

The picture in my head

simply too "marvellous"

        to ignore.

Lisa McCosh

Lisa McCosh
has chemical-free brown skin,
underarm hair,
and curves
in all the right places.

Lisa McCosh
carries
the scent of chai tea,
incense,
and fresh papaya body spray
    on her clothing.

Lisa McCosh is a vision
    resplendent,
even under neon lighting;
her short cropped hair
crying out for the softness of touch.

And Lisa McCosh
is the last person on earth
that Johnny should be calling a dyke
    every time I mention her name.

Lisa McCosh sits with me,
half an hour before
my first official Sanctuary Network meeting,
reads the first draft of my history speech,
and shows me how
to reword it
for maximum effect.

But sitting opposite Lisa,
    the only "maximum effect" I really grasp
is the chill-thrill every time she speaks to me
or stares in my direction;
and the bulge in my pants
every time she leans over.

By the time Lisa finishes scribbling her suggestions
into the margins of my work,
I look down at my writing
and start to feel pretty happy
about how it's shaping up.

But even more satisfying than that
is the feeling I get
every time
Lisa's big creamy eyes
connect with mine.

At those moments
all I feel
      is
"speechless".

Before the speech

Speech cards at the ready.
Palms tacky with sweat.
Fingers trembling.
I stand in front of the history class
and prepare myself to speak.

A traffic jam of chairs,
desks,
and tired looking students
stretches out before my eyes
right up to the back of the classroom
where Paddy and Johnny sit,
patiently waiting for me to begin.

Summoning up all the courage I can muster,
I lift back my shoulders
and open my mouth to speak.

My speech begins

'Indonesian soldiers raped my wife, burnt her with cigarettes and then shot her in the head. They forced me to watch everything. I begged for them to kill me too.'

These are the pain filled words of Domingos Gonzales, who lives today on Australia's doorstep, in the small country of East Timor.

In the summer of 1983, along with 287 other East Timorese, Domingos' wife was slaughtered in cold blood by the Indonesian army in the small town of Kraras.

The names of other victims include:
Antonio Bosi, aged 5, "shot";
Marcelino Soares, aged 56, "strangled";
Miguel Soares, aged 23, "shot";
Maria Gomes, aged 21, "Raped and drowned";
Kai Dos Anjos, aged 6 months, "shot".

These are the names of real human beings who have been crying out to Australia for help. But has Australia ever answered their call?

Mr Swaggert, classmates and invited guests,

You might be sitting there, wondering why I'm talking about East Timor when this assignment was meant to be about Australians and their great achievements throughout history.

But you see, the more I thought about this assignment, the more uncomfortable I felt about what I was being asked to do. The type of historical events I was being asked to study by Mr Swaggert seemed too glossy and nice. I felt like I was being asked to look at history through rose-coloured glasses. I felt like I was being asked to pick from a narrow band of history and then study it in a shallow way. And why? To make me more proud of being Australian? To make me into a true Aussie citizen?

I am not saying it's wrong to look at the big "achievements" in history, especially the ones that inspire us and make us feel proud. But I am saying that perhaps it's wrong to look at these 'achievements' by themselves as Mr Swaggert wants us to and not look at the other side of the coin; at our shortcomings and failures too.

In fact, the more I thought about it, the more dangerous I came to think this one sided approach to history was. For if history itself is complex, wouldn't you expect the study of history to be complex too?

This led me on to think about Australian history. I mean, haven't Australians failed as much as they succeeded in history? And if they have, isn't it important that my speech reflect this truth?

The answer I arrived at was "yes, it is important!"

In fact, in order to learn from the lessons of history, and not repeat the mistakes, I reckon it's essential.

Which brings me back to the topic of my speech: "Aussie sacrifices in history". To help me talk about this topic I've chosen to use East Timor as my backdrop. You see, Australia shares a rich history with East Timor which makes it the perfect place to explore the theme of "Aussie sacrifice". In particular, it's perfect because the history we share with each other is full of tales of proud sacrifice and shameful betrayal.

But before I get into the nuts and bolts of my talk, I just want to pause for a moment to share with you a quote from our Governor General, Sir William Deane, that relates to my topic.

Sir William Deane wrote that "a country's true historical greatness should never be measured by its achievements in the arts, sport, politics or science; it should be measured by the way is treats the least in its midst."

Classmates, guests, and Mr Swaggert,

my speech today looks at Australian sacrifice, betrayal and the way we treat the least in our midst. And the least in our midst most certainly include the East Timorese.

The rest of my presentation

After explaining Australia's history
with East Timor,
I conclude my speech
by introducing the class
to Paddy
and Johnny.

Paddy walks
to the front of the class
and begins to talk.

Within seconds,
the mood in the room
shifts from boredom
to interest;
as yawns disappear,
replaced by the straightening
of previously slouched backs.

By the time Paddy has finished,
half the girls are in tears,
Macro Lombardi is completely lost for words,
and Mr Swaggert is squirming in his seat.

Gloating at Swaggert's obvious distress,
I switch my gaze over to Johnny
who takes one look at my smirk
and shakes his head in disappointment.
Then,
instead of making his way
to the front of the class to sing,
as he was supposed to do,
Johnny simply packs up his guitar,
stands up
and walks straight out
the classroom door.

Johnny leaves,

 dragging my finale
            behind him.

Dressed down

'I can't believe you'd do that
to Paddy and me, mate!' Johnny shouts,
kicking the side of my banana lounge.

'Your speech was real smart, Pedro,
but it was also full of shit.
If I hadda known
you were gunna put down your teacher like that
I never would've come.
I saw the way you were trying
to get at him.
I heard your put downs.
Mate, haven't ya learned anything yet?
Even if you hate your teacher,
no one deserves to be treated
like that in front of others.
And for your info,
when you talk to people about East Timor
it's about winning them over,
not kicking them in the balls.'

Johnny turns around
and stamps off
towards the stairwell,
leaving me all alone.

A cold wind
blows across the rooftop
and for the next hour
I sit on my banana lounge
overtaken by the same feelings of anger
and disappointment I had
the day Dad left.

But this time
there's a difference.

This time the person to blame isn't my dad.

This time
the culprit
is me.

Scream

With Johnny long gone,
I balance myself
at the rooftop's edge,
close my eyes
and feel the rain on my skin
as it starts to fall
from the clouds above.

Tilting my head
    skywards,
the rain
sprinkle-falls
onto my open face
like holy water.

'Yes the rain is a blessing,'
I think to myself.
'It washes away all the filth.'

The weeping sky
    holds me
in its big moist arms;
wetting me
the whole way through.

Teetering on the brink,
I replay Johnny's angry words
over and over
in my head
until they slowly start to fade.

Capturing the feeling

Picking up my school bag
I run out of the rain
and into the stairwell.
Collapsing against the wall,
I take out my folder and pen.

Thinking about the cleansing rain outside,
I scribble down a few ideas
for a new poem,
but I don't know where to begin.
The things
I'm really wanting to say
feel all jammed up inside.

Memories,
    Johnny,
happiness,
pain,

        the rain.

How to go further?
    How to capture this feeling?

I suddenly remember Lisa McCosh
telling me once
how Sister McKenzie
was a well-known poet

and instantly
    I know what to do.

Help from above?

"Richmond Town".
    I think it's the best poem
I've ever written,
and it's all thanks to Sister McKenzie,
her weekly cups of tea,
and her demands for meticulous redrafting.
Sister McKenzie has the most amazing images
swimming round in her head.
(Hmm? I wonder how much of this poem
is actually mine?)

My poem: Richmond Town

Let the rain kiss
the old tannery sheds
decades worn but
          standing
on Flockhart Street
where forklifts scurry
like ants
moving pallets,
              blue painted,
      onto trucks

Let the rain kiss
the towering red brick walls
of the Carlton and United Brewery
and the Autumn wind
blowing the smell
of barley-hops
down Church Street
to the old bearded man
sitting
bottle-empty
in Citizens Park

Let the rain kiss
the rusted steel roof
of the wool sorting shed
on Burnley Street
where fleece is no longer tossed
across the grading table
and where the voice of the foreman
is no longer heard

Long deserted

Sign of
another age

Let the rain kiss
Richmond's Little Miss Saigon

and her long veranda walkways
stretching up Victoria Street,
where Asian grocery stalls
spill out on to the footpath;
restaurants perfume the street
with the scent of lemon grass
sesame oil
and fried bok choi;
        and the painted names
on shop windows
shout at those walking past:
Hai Phu butcher!
Phuoc Hung hot bread!
Hoa Hoa imports!
Let the rain kiss

Let the rain kiss
the bluestone lane ways
behind Victoria Street
where beeping garbage trucks
        lift green skip bins to the sky,
where effluent leaks from broken pipes,
and dope dealers
sell happiness by the gram

Let the rain kiss
the council workers
stop sign leaning
on Punt Rd,
gridlocking traffic,
and the concert posters
hastily slapped to cold stone walls

Let the rain kiss
the little plastic intercom,
never lonely for conversation,
at the Needle Exchange Office
on Lennox Street
where junkies
collect their cotton
syringes
and spoons

Let the rain kiss
the Richmond Hill's Food Centre
behind the Church of Saint Ignatius
where my Mother
loads the Mathew Talbot Soup Van
twice a week
before driving out
into a hungry night

A poor woman
too proud to ask for handouts herself

Let the rain kiss
the boom gates
editing people
in and out of GTV 9 studios
on Bendigo Street
Yes, let the rain kiss
this place
where stars rise
then fall
and where our thinking
is digitally remastered
behind closed doors

Let the rain kiss
the twisted neon tubing
that flickers to life at night
The "Nylex Clock"
*   glowing atop*
the malting silos
by the banks of the Yarra
And Little Audrey,
the "Skipping Girl",
jumping all night
over her rotating
*   fluorescent rope*

Let the rain kiss
the Corner Hotel
where shrewd buskers
can turn a profit

from the drunks
champagne spilling
onto the sidewalk

Let the rain kiss
all the places in Richmond
our feet have tread
and our eyes have touched
Wet with rain
Wet with sorrow
Wet with memory
Wet with joy and laughter
Let the rain pitter-patter fall
and let me fall too:
knee to chest
lip to ground
a thousand papal blessings
over this sacred town

Let the rain kiss
and cry no more
because the sky is tired of weeping

Let the rain kiss
with wet anointed lips
these places I now call home

Birthday preparations

I haven't seen Johnny
for five long weeks.

Sitting at my desk
late at night,
I fold the final draft
of my poem
into a neat square
and squeeze it
into a birthday card
I'd purchased
down at the Van Nguyen's grocery store.

Inside the card
is a short
handwritten message:

Dear Johnny,

You were right to be angry with me and I'm really sorry about
what I've done. Please believe me when I say I do care, both
about you and about East Timor. The poem I've written is my
gift to you. I thought you might be able to turn it into a song.
I hope you have a great birthday.

Your friend,

Pedro

Licking the envelope shut,
I climb into bed.

Sleep swallows up the night.

Chapter 4:

In the garden

Age 17:
Richmond

Johnny 11: 16

Riding the elevator
to the eleventh floor,
I look down
at the birthday card in my hand
and picture Johnny's face.

The elevator door slides open
and with a heavy feeling in my gut,
I step out into the dimly-lit corridor.

Reaching flat 16,
I knock on the security screen door
and listen to the thong slapping approach
of footsteps
from within.

Seconds later,
the front door
uncorks itself
like an old bottle of wine and
the stench of bad living
hits me square
in the face.

An overweight, middle-aged man
steps into view
scratching his armpit.

'What the hell do you want?'

The man yawns,
his mouth a mess
of tar-stained,
tic tac teeth.

'Well, don't just stand there,
what do ya want!' he repeats,
raising his voice.

'I'm here to see Johnny,' I say,
digging my hands deep
into my pockets.

The man looks at me
for a moment
before spitting out a reply,
'Shit, well ya better come in then.
Juan's told me all about you.
You're Pedro, right?
He's hiding in his room.
Maybe you can get the lazy bastard outta bed.'

The man,
who I assume is Johnny's white Australian uncle,
turns around
and yells out:
'GET UP JUAN,
YA LAZY PRICK!'

With my heart pumping,
I step into the flat
and head in the direction
of the man's angry
words
and flying spittle.

'YOU HEAR ME, JUAN?
GET OUTTA BED NOW
BEFORE I COME IN THERE
AND DRAG YA OUT!'

Johnny's tomb

Johnny's uncle's
ugly words
muffle and blur
as I step into Johnny's bedroom
and close the door
behind me
with a satisfying click.

Standing there
in the dreary darkness of Johnny's bedroom,
I reach out for a light switch.

The fluorescent tubing above my head
buzzes once
 then flickers to life;
each flash revealing
something new
in the room around me:

a poster of Che Guevara,

a weird painting of two weeping women,

and a wobbly old pile of books.

Curled up
on a mattress on the floor
under a tomb of bed sheets
is Johnny.

'Piss off Pedro,
leave me the fuck alone!'
Johnny says
 grunting displeasure,
 his head buried
under a pillow.

Standing there
in the musty
unventilated room,
I feel the chill of Johnny's words
and think about leaving.

But as I step towards the door
something on the other side
of the room
catches my eye.

Surrounded by broken tiles,
and assorted hand tools
is a massive mosaic
mounted
on a huge piece
of cement sheeting.

The sheer size of the thing,
simply staggering.

Johnny couldn't have made that,
could he?

I step closer
and find myself
gazing down
at what must be
Johnny's handiwork.

In the centre of the mosaic
is the image of an open grave.
And stepping out of the grave
is the figure
of a young woman
in a blood-stained dress
waving an East Timorese flag.
Off to the side
is a young boy,
running towards the woman with outstretched arms.
And across the clear blue sky
in red letters
are the tiled words:
LAZZARO RISING
VIVA TIMOR LESTÉ!

Crouching down,
    I run my fingers
over the surface of Johnny's creation,

'Johnny isn't getting rid of me that easy,'
I think to myself,
'not on his birthday.'

I run my fingers
over the surface of the tiles
one more time,

    remembering

        Johnny

    all those months ago,

kneeling and weeping

on the Cathedral's

dusty mosaic floor.

Rising to life

I knew Johnny got stoned
from time to time,
he told me so,
but I'd never seen it
up close.

Wrapped in his bed sheets
like some weird embalmed mummy,
Johnny drags himself up
onto the edge of the bed
and pushes the bong
on the floor
underneath a pile of clothing.

Johnny's eyes are sunken pools of oil,
 —drug-fucked
and stupefied —
a quagmire of misery.

I sit down
beside Johnny on his bed
and pass him
his birthday present.

'Happy birthday, Johnny,' I say.

Half-stoned,
Johnny sits there
and tries to unwrap the present
placed on his knee.
But eventually,
he gives up
and hands the present
back to me
unopened.

At his request,
I unwrap the present
and read out the contents,
hopeful the words inside

might help to revive
our struggling friendship.

I read the words slowly
and with care;
ending with a final:
'I'm sorry, mate,
I really am.'

'Nah, forget about it, Brother,
That was a shit of a day.
I'm the one who should be fucking sorry.
I've never gone to a high school before.
Seeing all those students
just fucked with me head.'

Johnny reaches out,
grabs his pouch of tobacco
and starts to roll a smoke.

'And thanks for the poem, P J.
It's fucking great.
I'm stoked you remembered
me birthday.'

About time

'Get dressed
and grab your guitar Johnny,
you're coming out with me today.
I'm not letting you stay in here;
not on your birthday.'

I open the bedroom curtains
and flood the room with sunlight.
Johnny squints and groans,
but after a few seconds
he realises I mean business
and reluctantly starts to get dressed.

'That mosaic you're making
is awesome Johnny,' I say,
trying to make conversation
as Johnny fumbles
with his shoelaces.

Johnny just grunts.

Finally,
dressed and ready to go,
I hand Johnny his guitar case
and guide his unresponsive body
through the bedroom door.

'It's about time you got outta bed
ya lazy bastard,' Johnny's uncle snaps,
as we step through the doorway.
'You better go busking today Juan
or I'll smash that fucking thing
you're making
in your room.
Do ya hear me, Juan?
You better start paying your way again
or your Dad...'

'...Você abandona Papai
fora disto!' Johnny exclaims,
turning around
clearly agitated.

I grab Johnny's arm
and push him firmly
towards the exit.

I push him hard;
worried by the murderous look
on his face.

Crispy Pata

Out in the corridor,
bruised and wounded
by Johnny's uncle's words,
some things about Johnny
finally start to add up.

I start to understand
why Johnny never invited me
over to his place,
and why he
always seemed so pleased
when my Mum
asked him over
for dinner —

even when Crispy Pata

was on the menu.

A question

Riding the elevator
to the ground floor,
I look over at Johnny
and realise I've never seen him
like this before:
so flat,
so quiet
so removed,
so compliant.

Like a helium balloon
after the party is over,
Johnny had completely
lost his vigour,
buoyancy and bounce.

Dragging his feet on the concrete
he turns and asks me a question,
'Where ya taking me, Pedro?'

I let the question
hang in the air
for a moment.
Coming to a stop,
I point my finger
out in front of me.

'To a garden party, Johnny,' I say.

Johnny looks across the car park
to the chainmesh fence
of the community garden
and moans.

'Johnny, I made my Mum
a promise, remember?
But I can't do this alone.
Anyway,
Mum's expecting you;
she's made you a cake.'

I move forward
and Johnny follows,
muttering swear words
under his breath.

We leave the shelter of the tower's shade
and step through the garden's gate;
    out into the extravagance of the sun.

In the garden

Straight staked winter vegetables,
borderline perfect
in weedless plots of manicured earth.

Ugly car tyres
sprouting tuffs of green foliage.

Caged garden beds
warning intruders
to "stay out!"

A dish-rack gate
swaying in the morning breeze.

Big painted letters
hung from the perimeter fence,
spelling out the words, EDEN GARDENS,
     reflecting hope inwards.

The sculpture of a woman
made entirely of old car parts;
her skeleton veined by shoots
of climbing bougainvillea.

Other gardens,
tangled labyrinths of snarling green,
snapping at CDs
dangled from string
overhead.

A communal garden shed,
     plastered
with "crime stopper" posters
in five different languages.

A wooden seat
carved into the shape of the moon.

And a scarecrow
dressed in a Collingwood jumper,
its hair

a plume of magpie feathers,
heckling at those passing by.

All around us
a garden.

All around us
so much more.

All around us
an ocean of human endeavour:
bent backs,
calloused hands
words of advice —

    green waves of creation

dotted

    by the flotsam of life.

The Cake

With our senses bombarded
by the strange sights around us,
we finally find Mum
waiting for us
beside a weed infested vegetable plot
in the middle of the garden.

'Happy Birthday, Johnny,' Mum says,
giving Johnny
a generous kiss
on the cheek,
before removing a box of matches
from her hip pocket.

Mum hands Johnny
a sweet smelling passionfruit cake
and lights up
the candles
on top.

Then, with a nod of her head,
Mum and me
break into a song,
singing "Happy Birthday",
much to the surprise
of the three old men,
smoking and playing cards
around a little green table
three plots back.

Pulling weeds

'This garden plot is for Evie,' Mum says,
pointing down
at the thick matting of weeds
directly behind her.
'But Evie needs your help, ok?
You boys are very good to help her.'

With our stomachs full
of tasty passionfruit cake,
Johnny looks at my Mum
as she hands us each a spade
and smiles.

'Make sure you put the tools
back in the shed when you're done,'
Mum says
before wishing us 'good luck'
and heading off
towards
her own plot
at the back of the enclosure.

'Relax,' I whisper to Johnny
as Mum walks away,
'You don't have to do
any gardening, mate.
Leave the hard work to me.'

Johnny peers down at the shovel
in his hands
and lets out a sigh of relief

Sitting down
on the ground,
Johnny watches me
as I get to work.

My spade
strikes down at the dirt,
loosening roots.

Then,
stooping over
I yank hard
 at the stubborn weeds
beneath my feet.

The work is tiring
and after fifteen minutes of ferocious weeding
my t-shirt becomes wet
with perspiration.

'Hey Pedro,' Johnny pipes up from behind me,
'what the fuck
am I here for again?
I'm no gardener you know.'

Grateful for the distraction,
I turn to face Johnny
and tap the side of his guitar case
with the tip of my spade.
'I never said you had to garden, Johnny.
All I said,
is that I needed your help.
Mum told me yesterday that Evie liked music
even more than gardening.
So that makes you the friggin' entertainment, Johnny,
didn't I tell you that?
You're here
to sing her some goddamned songs.'

Evie arrives

Five-year-old Evie
finally arrives in the community garden
and is guided down the main path
by old Mr Santiago.

Walking hand in hand,
the pair stops
directly in front of me and Johnny.

Dressed in a light blue dress,
her hair tied back in a ponytail,
Evie lets go of Mr Santiago's hand
and skips
over to me.

'Gimme five, Pedro,' she says
holding up her palm.

Giving me some skin,
Evie then turns towards Johnny,
sitting on the ground
and asks,
'Why you looking so sad, scary monster?'

Evie's words have an immediate effect.

'WHO... SAYS...   I'M... SAD!'
Johnny smiles and shouts
in his best monster's voice.

Johnny then removes his guitar
from its case
and immediately starts
to belt out a tune:
'They call me the music monster,
But...   I'm...   not... so... sad...

I'M... JUST...

    HUNGRY!'

Evie squeals with delight
as Johnny reaches out
to tickle her tummy.

And when the tickling finally stops,
Evie plonks herself down on the ground,
mesmerised by Johnny.
Evie begs him to keep on singing.

Johnny gladly obliges.

And as I kneel back
in the dirt,
and return to the inglorious work
of "pulling" out weeds,
Johnny sings song after song
"pulling" out happiness instead.

Reinvigorated

The perfect tonic
for being stoned
has got to be
a smiling five-year-old girl.

After singing her a stack of songs,
Johnny spends the rest of his time
with Evie
exploring the community garden.

At one point
I watch with surprise
as Evie pushes Johnny to the ground
and jumps on top of him,
whooping laughter.

Later on,
I lift my eyes from the ground,
only to see Evie
sitting atop Johnny's shoulders —
Johnny spinning her
around and around
in dizzying circles.

And then
as a grand finale,
I watch with interest as Johnny
flings himself to the ground
time and time again
trying to catch a runaway chicken
from the garden's chook shed.

Standing behind him,
Evie claps and cheers
as Johnny finally catches
the poor terrified bird.

'It's good to have you back, Johnny,'
I think to myself
as I watch Evie reach out
and pat the chicken
trapped in Johnny's arms.

'It's good to have you back.'

Preparing the way for the seed

Bound up
by tough threads of knotted kokuya;

cluttered
with clumps of back-breaking clay;

shielded from prying hands
by patches of bindi-eyes
and stinging nettles;

this hostile surface of earth,
—however plump with promise—
was always going to take
some breaking.

Satisfied

After two-and-a-half hours of digging
and weeding
I look down at Evie's plot and realise
I'm only a quarter done.

Yet,
despite the slow progress,
and the blister wet handle in my hands,
I can't help but feel a little satisfied.

Outside in the sun

with Mum smiling again,

Johnny back to his old self

and little Evie laughing with delight;

life almost seems good.

I look down
at the growing pile of uprooted weeds
by my feet
—pulled out with the effort
of my own two hands—
and even manage a smile.

Mr Santiago

Mr Santiago's
on a pretty good wicket
I reckon.

On Fridays
he gets his groceries
hand delivered
to his flat's front door by yours truly.

Then, on most other afternoons,
he sits beside his garden plot,
reading books,
while my Mum brings him
hot cups of green tea
and friendly conversation.

And on Saturdays,
his garden plot
gets weeded
by Johnny,
"I'm not a gardener",
Lazzaro,
who's suddenly found
that he's got a "green thumb".

In defence,
Johnny says, 'he's a legend Pedro,
back in East Timor
he was a part of Fretilin.
Dad's in Fretilin, Pedro.
If he was here,
my Dad would fucking love him!'

Mum,
on the other hand,
says Mr Santiago
deserves my respect,
because Mr Santiago,
  in her humble opinion,
'is the wisest man at Eden Towers.
Back in East Timor,
he was a doctor, Pedro,
    a doctor!'

At the end of the day

Every Saturday at the community garden
before Johnny and me leave
—our jobs done,
Evie gone—
Mr Santiago waves us over
to his garden bed.

Sitting in front of us,
grinning mischievously,
Mr Santiago always commends us
on our good work.

Then,
just like clockwork,
Mr Santiago makes me read out
his Question of the week:
before allowing us to go.
I humour Mr Santiago
out of politeness, I guess.

But for Johnny,
it's different.

Every week,
Johnny hangs on
to Mr Santiago's questions
like my Mum
hangs on to her rosary beads
at Mass—

meditating on their meaning.

Question of week I

Mr Santiago
passes me
his Question of the week
on a slip of paper.

Clearing my throat
and looking across at Johnny,
I read the words out loud:

'What is it that makes a gardener truly happy;
the beauty of the plants growing in his garden
or the health of his soil
underneath?'

The meeting

At the first
Sanctuary Network meeting in July
Johnny and me
sit with Sister McKenzie,
working out plans
for participation
at the upcoming
Moon Lantern Festival.

Sitting in the conference room
of the Richmond Community Health Centre
Johnny and me
come up with heaps
of ideas:

'What about making show bags, Sister?'

'What about doing a dramatic re-enactment?'

'What about selling East Timorese food?'

Sister McKenzie
nods her head,
trying not to dash our hopes,
but in the end
she's the boss.

In the end,
she decides what we'll do.

As the clock strikes ten,
and our meeting draws to a close,
the details of participation
have been locked into place:

an information stall,

a petition,

a tin for donations

and one small concession for Johnny

    —the opportunity
to sing.

Mr Santiago's gift

On my birthday,
Mr Santiago gives me
an old book about plants,
their names
and the way they grow.

'Imee says you write poetry, Pedro.
But I think you write better
if you know the words of nature,' Mr Santiago explains
flicking open the book.

I read out some of the words
Mr Santiago points to
with his finger
as he navigates through the pages:

'himalayan marigold',
'frangipani',
'snapdragon',
and 'minnetonka rhododendron'.

'See Pedro,' Mr Santiago says,
weirdly excited by the sounds
coming out of my mouth,
'sometimes a plant's name
more beautiful than the plant itself.'

A quote

Back in my room,
I open Mr Santiago's gift
to the first page
and notice that
Mr Santiago has written something —
a quote.

Dear Pedro,

'A garden is like those pernicious machineries
which catch a man's coat-skirt or his hand,
and draw in his arm, his leg,
and his whole body to irresistible destruction.'
(Ralph Waldo Emerson)

Happy Birthday,

Jose Santiago

Birthday

Stepping out
onto the freezing cold rooftop,
my body shivering,
I look over
at the warm welcoming face
of Johnny
and instantly
forget the chill.

'Happy birthday brother,' he calls out,
walking over
and giving me a bear hug
before directing me over
to the large birthday present
sitting on the ground,
'it's from Imee too.'

Bending over,
I remove the present's wrapping
and look down
at the gift inside:
a handmade
Djembe drum.

My jaw drops to the floor.

'This is awesome,' I say,
shoving the drum between my legs
and beating out a steady rhythm.
'I can't believe
you got my Mum to help you,
it's awesome.'

I spend the next few minutes
 drumming happily away
until a strange looking
bunch of balloons
drifts into view
next to Johnny's feet.

'So did my Mum help to pay
for those birthday balloons as well?' I ask,
smiling cheekily.

Johnny looks down
at the inflated balloons
hovering near his feet
and starts to laugh.

'Nah, they were fucking free.
Got 'em down
at the needle exchange office.
Shit,
the things I do for me mates.
It's wasn't easy blowin' them up,
let me tell you,
those connies are slippery little things.'

I step over
and kick one of the inflated condoms
high into the air:

'Well at least you only filled them
with hot air, Johnny,' I say.
'At least you didn't
fill them with something "more solid".'

Johnny crumples to the floor,
laughing.

'How can you be so sure, brother?' he bawls.

    'How can you be so sure?'

Moon lantern preparations

Johnny,
Evie
and me
sit in a room full of volunteers
at the Richmond Community Health Centre
and focus on the job at hand.

Crammed around tables,
singing nursery rhymes,
we do the painstaking work
of making crepe paper lanterns
for the upcoming festival;
                  our scissors slashing melodies to air.

Johnny's skilful hands
guide Evie's
as he teaches her the fine art
 of cutting,
tracing
positioning and pasting with care

                  and laughter.

After a few practise runs
Evie then goes it alone,
successfully pasting
her first panel into position
before pushing a candle
into place.

Evie's first lantern
brings squeals of delight —

her smile

lighting up the whole room.

Question of week II

Mr Santiago
passes me
his Question of the week
on a slip of paper.

Clearing my throat
and looking across at Johnny,
I read the words out loud:

'Which of these
is the greatest gift of the garden:
the food that is harvested
or the restoration of the five senses?'

A doctor's work

Peruvian needle grass,
Bone weed,
Bridal creeper,
Paterson's curse,
Milk thistle
    and Burr.

Scalpels for fingers
I incise the earth,
          extracting the tumours
          before they can spread.

But this cancer
is too malignant
too chronic,
    too strong.

This surgery
too clumsy —

cosmetic.

Looking down at the holes
now pockmarking earth,
my black-stained fingers
go to work
folding the dirt
back into each
and every open wound;

    visible mending.

'Spade please,' I say,
sizing up
a final knob
of Bone weed
in the garden's guts.

My five-year-old assistant
places a thick
wooden handle
into the palm of my hand.

A doctor's work is never done.

Question of week III

Mr Santiago
passes me
his Question of the week
on a slip of paper.

Clearing my throat
and looking across at Johnny,
I read the words out loud:

'Why be a gardener
when despite your best efforts
weeds continue to grow?'

Hard prune

Mr Santiago's "odd jobs"
never seem to end.
Handing me a set of pruning shears
we march
to the centre of the community garden
and stop in front
of a tired looking,
leafless
old tree.

'This apple tree planted here long time ago, Pedro,
when we start the garden.
We call it the "gathering tree",' Mr Santiago explains,
'but no fruit come last year.
We fix that, understand?
We give it a hard prune.'

The crazy old man
instructs me to hack deep
into the tree's limbs,
so deep
I start to wonder
whether the tree
will even survive.

I cut off the dead wood
and disease;
create space
for the air to circulate;
and step back to
look at my handiwork.

'Don't lose faith, Pedro, you see,
Hard prune bring much fruit.
Hard prune,
like hard love;

    only way new life grows.'

Sayings

I add Mr Santiago's new saying
about 'hard love'
being the 'only way things will grow'
next to all his other sayings:

'best fertilizer is the gardener's shadow',

'best watering come from gardener's sweat ...'

Tell me Mr Santiago,

    do you make all this shit up?

Companion planting

Maxine Rendell,
the project manager at the garden,
comes up to me one day
and gives me this article
about organic gardening
and companion planting.

With Evie's plot
now freshly weeded
and springtime
fast approaching,
Maxine reckons
companion planting
is the way to go.

I read the article
and learn
how tomatoes
grow well near basil,

beans can use corn stalks to climb,

and mint repels cabbage moths
before they land.

Looking up
from the page,
I stare out over the garden
and watch Evie
as she climbs
like a jasmine
vine
all over Johnny's shoulders.

Companion planting?

        It's got to work.

The evidence
    is staring me right in the face.

Water fights

The garden hose
held by a five-year-old's hands
can be a dangerous weapon;
capable
of spraying
more than water,
but laughter
and mayhem in every direction.

'Look out, Evie!'

'Johnny's filling the bucket!'

Moon lantern festival

Under the all seeing eye
of the towers
we line up
row upon row.

The PA crackles to life
as we lift our bamboo poles
to the sky.

Lanterns sway,
soft light spreads,
silken tassels whip the wind.

 This is the start
of our Moon Lantern Festival —

where young and old,
Somali and Greek,
Timorese and Turk,
Buddhist and Sikh,
Man and woman
come together
in a show
of unity.

Unity

is African dancing classes,
     fruit carving lessons,
hair braiding workshops
                    and laughter

Unity

is a smorgasbord of food
     from around the world:
     pappadums and couscous,
noodle soups and muufo,
     deep-fried bananas and Mam.

Unity

is a rainbow of costumes
gathered
under a firework framed sky:
floral sarongs and burqas,
cotton hijabs and jodhpurs
turbans and pantaloons.

Unity

is the festival stage,
showcasing local talent:
African drummers;
Vietnamese Hip-hop dancers;
a West Papuan Choir;
and Johnny
"the activist"
Lazzaro.

Unity.

Is it really possible?

Working the stall

Five Hundred dollars
was a lot to raise
at our Sanctuary Network stall
in just one night.

That's what Sister McKenzie says.

Johnny agrees,
although he reckons
it was largely thanks to him.

'All that money came in
after I sang,' Johnny insists.

Johnny's got no idea.

The truth is
that it was
Sister McKenzie
who sat all night at the stall
while Johnny and me
went out
"to spread the word".

And it was Sister McKenzie
who was willing to talk
to anyone passing by
and anyone who would listen.

But then again,
perhaps it doesn't matter
who gets the credit.

The important thing
is that 500 dollars
    is 500 dollars;
and that's pretty good going
in anyone's books.

After the festival

'Asian Prick!'

Knife flash.

The gang of Suddies presses in tight,
eyes gleaming.

Stairwell floor.

Falling...

Hand clasping neck

    warm sticky mess

fingertip leakage.

This concrete,

so cold...

gut slammed,

a black hand

my wallet ripping.

Shadow shapes blur

to darkness...

    Silence...

BRIGHT LIGHT!

Johnny's face

blood stained

hazing to focus

'Call a fucking ambulance!

    Do it! Do it fucking now!'

Nine

The Silver-Top taxi
pulls into St Vincent's car park
and Johnny and me
climb into the back seat.

Waiting in the front seat is Mum,
    her face wet with tears.

'Lennox Street,' Mum says,
turning briefly towards the driver,
before shifting her undivided attention
back to me.

Resting my head
on Johnny's shoulder,
the stitches on my neck
start to throb
as the taxi turns into Victoria Parade.

Two blocks later,

    I'm crying.

Mum climbs
into the back seat,
ignoring the driver's protests
and pulls me into her arms

Caressing my cheek
with her soft, warm hands,
she whispers into my ear:

Nine stitches,
Nine words:

'That's my boy, you just let it all out.'

Not so bad

This sun on my back
    is not so bad.

This thawing out.

This petal-like turning
    of face
to catch the sun.

It's not so bad
this wind
feathering
pollen to air,
as springtime declares.

It's not so bad

to watch green buds swell
    then split

as in this garden
I sit.

It's not so bad.

It's not so bad.

Quote of the week

Mr Santiago
passes me
not a Question
but a Quote of the week
on a slip of paper.

Clearing my throat
and looking across at Johnny,
I read the words out loud:

'You can bury a lot of troubles digging in the dirt.'

Chapter 5:

Falling and Rising

Age 18:
Richmond

Falling

On the dark side of the tower
where nothing much grows

they find Johnny's body —

a mangled mess
        of blood
and broken bones.

Sergeant Clifford says
'the incident'
happened after midnight;

        his death,
'instantaneous'.

Sergeant Clifford says
Johnny had a letter
        in his hand.

Sergeant Clifford says
it must have been suicide.

But Sergeant Clifford
doesn't know shit!

I mean,
how could my best mate leave me
without even saying goodbye?

Tell me Johnny

'Tell me Johnny,
what were
you doing
up there so late at night?'

'Were you emptying your head
of nightmares?
22 storeys high,
"being" not "staying" alive?'

'Were you drunk,

stoned?'

'Or did you simply slip?'

'Tell me, Johnny,

cause I need to know.

    It wasn't suicide,

was it?'

A moving mosaic

Johnny's uncle fills the doorway
with his fat ugly frame.

'Piss off the lot of ya!' he yells,
spitting out
his words like bullets.

Paddy ignores the abuse
and barges his way
into the flat.

'Show us the way,' Paddy says,
giving me a nod.

Under the angry gaze
of Johnny's uncle,
we make our way
into Johnny's bedroom
and seize what we came for:
Johnny's mosaic
and his battered old guitar.

By the time
we leave the flat
Johnny's uncle is screaming,
'I'll call the fucking cops!'

Sister McKenzie swings around
and glares,
'Then tell the police
you were burgled by a nun,'
she snaps back.

Fernando Gonzales,
standing in the corridor,
readjusts his grip
under one end
of heavy mosaic
and smiles at the good Sister.

'Keep it coming,' Paddy orders,
waving us towards the lift
'steady as you go.'

Lazzaro Rising

Two star-pickets,

a sledge hammer

and some wire.

That's all we need.

Working as a team
we erect Johnny's mosaic
in the middle of the community garden,
underneath the shade
of the gathering tree.

Then,
with our work complete,
we join hands,
bow our heads
and listen to
Sister McKenzie's prayer.

'Lazzaro Rising,
Viva Timor Lesté,' she begins,
'Dear God, let these words of Johnny
one day become our reality.
May his spirit rise up
to Heaven
and may his spirit
keep rising up
in us.
Amen.'

The ceremony

After Sister McKenzie's prayer
we scatter Johnny's ashes.

Sister McKenzie then performs
the official blessing
before inviting people forward
to speak.

Words!
    Words!
Words!

Stepping out
in front of the small crowd
 —angry,
hurt and
confused—
I stare across at little Evie
and watch as she
buries her face
in the folds
of her mother's black dress.

'I couldn't write a speech,' I say,
'I could only write this poem.
But I reckon it's what Johnny
would've wanted.
Vive Timor Lesté Brother!'

My poem: Words for a funeral

Words.
Limp words.
Polished and scrubbed words.
Whispered words.
Angry words.
Religious words.
Well-meant words.
And haemorrhaged words,
*   poured out on the floor.*

Words
after the death of a person
are never enough

Words can never
*   know a man,*
mourn a man,
*   thank a man*
or hold a man in arms that won't let go.

Words catch and cling to your throat
like cigarette smoke
in a crowded room,
or like bread eaten too thick,
*   too quick*
*   and without water.*

Words fill up the spaces
left by the dead
but words are never enough;
*   words are never enough.*

Words
come from priests,
neighbours, friends,
and brothers
but rarely
from the mouth
of the little child

left behind —
the one who stands
pressed in tight
against the warmth of her mother's leg.

Words come and go
Words come and go
    in and out
like waves upon the sand.

But as you lie awake at night
feeling the aftershock still
you know the tsunami comes.
Alone in your room,
with the lights out,
you wait for the surge to hit
and wash away all the goddamned noise!
A giant wave of salted tear
    to smash
        and break upon your shore

and leave you floating
    adrift

in that *silent* space

      in that *wordless* space

    now damp

  with memory.

Viva Timor Lesté!

In August 1999,
East Timor holds a referendum
on its future
and somehow,
despite the intimidation,
the East Timorese people
vote in favour
of independence.

Days later,
I watch on the TV
as violence
and destruction erupt.
Thousands die.

Dili burns to the ground.

But by late September
Australian peacekeepers
move into the capital, Dili,
and order is restored.

Viva Timor Lesté!

It's the most heart-wrenching two months ever.

Viva Timor Lesté!

Johnny,

how I wish you were here.

Some people say

The pavement cracked
where Johnny's body had landed
and some people say
that you can fit
your entire hand
through the gap.

But I don't like listening
to what some people say.

I remove the little bag
of grass seeds
from my pocket
and wipe the sweat
from my brow.

Bending down,
I don't even see a crack.

All I see is an opening;

An opening calling out

    to be filled.

Chapter 6:

The taste of apple

Age 18:
Colac

New Year's Eve, 1999

Perched up here
on this rooftop,
with a stubby
of lukewarm beer,
toes folded over concrete,
I can almost hear
the sudden drawing in of breath
as the clock strikes twelve
and midnight slams its drunken fist
into the city's underbelly.

Gut-winded
doubled over
and moaning
the city
exhales,
marvels at the miracle of its own survival,
then stumbles
without grace
into a new millennium.

Down on the streets below
horns hoot,
lips lock
tongues collide
and New Year's resolutions are sworn
under the light
of a beer-swill moon.

Y2K

Despite all the hype
and all the predictions of digital disaster,
as the twenty-first century reveals its face

tragedy does not strike,

the Y2K bug does not bite

and planes do not fall from the sky.

Society brushes
the dust
of the past
from its shoulders
and steps out
    without regret
into the future.

New Year's resolution

Fireworks

spangle the sky.

Explosions

glitter-weep

then die,

while I

stand 22 storeys high

thinking of nothing
                but Johnny tonight.

'I miss you,
you mad bastard!' I cry

raising my stubby to the sky

    to catch

the ghost of Johnny's sigh:

    'Be alive,
    be alive.'

Bank Job

Halfway through
my job interview
it hits me –
all the places
I would rather be
than here:

studying creative writing at university,
working in East Timor as a volunteer,
making music in a band,
or changing the world
—one activist step
at a time.

But as the bank manager smiles,
clasping my hand in his,
I know my fate is sealed.

Walking home,
I picture
how happy
Mum will be
on hearing
my "good news".

I am homeward bound

                wound up inside

a knot of intestinal mourning.

A new identity

Behind the closed doors
of my bedroom
I remove
the bank issued shirt
from its
plastic
 packaging

pick up
the accompanying tie

and squeeze myself
into my new identity.

Standing in front
of the mirror
I tug at the collar
strangling my neck
and try to smile
—just as the
customer service lady
had shown me.

'Good morning, sir,'
                I practise to myself
     face frowning,
'can I be of assistance?'

'May I help you miss?'
                I ask,
     my voice a tunnel of wind.

'Good afternoon sir,' I say,
                stifling a yawn.

Shaking my head
in frustration,
I remove the cotton noose of tie
from around my neck
and throw it
 at the mirror.

'Why don't you just piss off and
use the ATM!'

My mouth sprays spittle

across the room

    and in the smudged reflection of the mirror

I finally

 manage

a smile.

Too...

These bank wages
are too small.

This flat we live in
is too claustrophobic.

These trips
to work
on tram
and bus
everyday
take too long.

This grin
hanging on my face
like an oil painting
is too forever.

This effort
to save money
for university
is too hard.

But my Mum's
constant
words of
support
are
way
too...

too...

...well chosen.

Weekend relief

I am knees to dirt
        weeding

I am troubled thoughts
and feelings;
buried
under soil
and work
and hay.

I am spade to ground
earth turning,
midday sun
back-burning
and seedlings
budding closer to bouquet.

I am sweat on brow
quick-dripping
and these young hands
grass ripping

I am

    I am

I am a mantra of human movement

    I am a living
garden prayer

I am
 right here

    I am
    right now

I am

        —present

The tree of knowledge

'Hard prune
bring much fruit.
I tell you so, Pedro.'

It's early Saturday morning
and the familiar voice of Mr Santiago
draws me out
of my gardener's trance.

I drop my spade,
stand up
and watch Mr Santiago
as he steps
towards me
past a wiry clump
of mustard grass.

Reaching my side,
he bows his head once
before extending
a little wicker basket
in my direction.

Inside the basket
is a freshly picked pile of apples
from the gathering tree.

'These apples for you, Pedro.'

Bowing my head in gratitude
I take the basket
from Mr Santiago's hands
and gaze down at
the rich red apples.

In the middle of the basket,
jammed between two of the apples,
is an envelope with my name scribbled on it
in my mother's
handwriting.

I grab the envelope
and open it up
to reveal
a train ticket
—destination
    Colac.

Mr Santiago gives me a smile
then leaves me
with some parting words of wisdom:

'Better you eat the apple, Pedro
than the apple eat at you.'

The bag over my shoulder

I place
Mr Santiago's rich red apples
into a shoebox,
wrap the shoebox in
 red cellophane
and voila!
—a present for Dad.

In my duffel bag
I place a change of clothing,
toiletries,
my journal,
and a copy of Dad's address in Colac.

Slipping my wallet
into
my pocket,
I pick up the train ticket
from the desk
and give my bedroom
one last scan
for anything
that I might have forgotten.

Ignoring the lingering doubts
in the back
of my mind,
I take a final
deep
breath
before swinging the bag
over my shoulder,
flicking the hair
out of my eyes
and picking up
the guitar case
from the floor.

Stepping into the lounge room,
Mum stops me
in my tracks,
        places
a big wet kiss
on my forehead
and wraps her arms around my waist.

'Good luck, Pedro,' she says.
'Good luck.'

Train trip

The world
outside
the window
is a flickering
blur
of traffic lights,
graffiti covered walls,
and urban sprawl.

But as the early morning train
to Colac
reaches
the countryside,
the land suddenly changes
to a flat vista
    of cheerless spinifex,

    tired fence posts

and dusty yellow fields.

Resting my head
on the cool clear glass,
the shudder
and grind
of the carriages
beats on
and on
and on
into a rhythm —

a lullaby.

My Eyelids

grow heavy

and my mind

slowly fades

into dreaming.

Stone walls

Waking up
somewhere past Winchelsea,
my eyes hit the countryside
with a slap.

I stare out
the train window
at an alien landscape;
my eyes mesmerized
by the long
stone walls
stretching out
over the fields
in every direction.

One of the walls
snakes an unbroken path
alongside
the speeding train
for what feels like
twenty minutes straight.

Reading the baffled look
on my face,
the old lady sitting opposite me
stops her knitting
and speaks:

'Those walls
were made by convicts,
you know.
Mile after mile.
They outlasted my parents
and they'll probably
outlast
you and me.'

For the rest
of the train trip
I gaze out
the window
in amazement—

finding hope
in the thought
that something
so goddamned enduring
could be built
by a bunch
of outcasts.

Rushing back

It's the truth, you know,
plain and simple.

Johnny's name is no longer poised
on the tip of my tongue.

He rarely
even enters
my dreams
anymore.

But sitting
in Memorial Park
in Colac,
waiting for the bus
to take me
out of town,
memories of Johnny
come rushing back in.

Maybe its the
 two
seagulls,
feather-puffing
and squawking over a piece
of bread
on the footpath,
that turn my thoughts back to Johnny.

I don't really know.

All I know
is that parading in front of me,
"bigger-than-Texas",
the seagulls,
entrance me
with
their
show.

At the bus stop

So many times I have tried
to capture the essence of Johnny
on a page
in a poem
or a song,
but the words have always eluded me.

But with my imagination
sparked
by the seagull's prancing,
I suddenly feel the urge
to try once more
to capture Johnny
in the words of a song.

Pulling Johnny's guitar
out of its case,
I sit at the bus stop
and strum out
the only two chords I'm any good at,
wondering if
some decent lyrics
might somehow appear.

Humming a melody
over the top of the notes
I close my eyes and picture
Johnny's face.

But every time
I open my mouth to sing
a load of meaningless
crap comes out.

I feel like a wanker
and a fraud.

The words I sing
are too forced,
too neat,

too tidy
and a dishonour
to my good friend's name.

'Three chords and the truth,'
I think to myself.
That's what Johnny use to say.
That's what Johnny would expect.
'Three chords and the truth.'

The truth —

whatever the hell that means.

Two chords and the truth

Happy with the melody
in my head,
I put down
my guitar,
open up my journal
and start to write down
as many honest thoughts
as I can
about Johnny.

It's hard to do
and the results disturb me,
but in the midst
of my struggle
for truthfulness
the idea for a song
gradually
starts to emerge.

It's a song
that's brutally honest.

It's a song
as much about me
as him.

It's a song
written with
two chords,
not three.

It's a
song I label
"Stone".

Stone (lyrics in the Appendix)

Listening in

The bus
from Colac
drops me off
on the outskirts
of town
next to an old
dilapidated
milking shed.

As the bus
drives away
in a cloud of dust,
I try to get
my bearings
by looking down
at the hand drawn map
in my fingertips.

Five minutes later
I'm heading north
on foot
towards my destination —
       Mahonys Road.
Walking along,
I try to distract myself
from thoughts of Dad
by listening
to the unfamiliar sounds
of the countryside:

the gravel-crunch
of my boots
on the open road;

the chortle
of magpies
fence post watching
as I pass;

the rustle
of wind
through the long dry grass;

and the distant rumble
of thunder
from the big fat clouds
on the horizon.

Walking along
I find distraction
and a touch of peace
in these rich
distinctive
sounds—

in these sounds
so free
and
so giving.

The farm

Walking past
paddocks
sprinkled with cows
it comes as a shock
when I finally reach
a big stand of pine trees
and a large sign
that reads:

COLAC
CHRISTMAS TREE
FARM
360 MAHONEYS ROAD

The scent of pine needles
floats on the air,
blanketing out
the competing smells of cow manure.
The pine makes everything seem fresher,
cleaner
and more vibrant.

I breathe in deep,
savouring the moment
until a strange thought
jolts me back to reality.

Pulling out the journal
from my bag,
I double check the details
of my dad's address
against the property number
on the sign.

My jaw drops.

The two numbers
are identical.

'You gotta be joking,'
I think to myself.

'Dad can't live here,

can he?'

Every step I take

Standing at the top
of the road,
I stare down
through the pine trees
and lightly falling rain
at the small weatherboard house
in the distance.

Adjusting my shirt
and running my fingers
through my damp hair,
I step forward.

Each step I take
draws me further
and further
down the tightening
chute
of driveway
and closer to
the point of no return.

My heart beats faster
and faster,
my mouth turns to dust
and my hands
dig deeper into their pockets.

When I finally reach
the front door,
I open up
my duffle bag
and somehow
manage
to drag Dad's present out
without dropping it.

'You can do this,' I mumble to myself,
forcing
my trembling hands

to knock on the door
to announce my arrival.

'You can do this,'

knocking again,

this time

much louder

and much harder.

Naughty, not nice

Muffled sounds
sharpen
to audible speech.

Quick moving feet
pad
an approach.

A rusty hinge
creaks.

The front door swings opens.

And through
a flywire screen
the face
of a stranger
stares up at me —
the open
freckled face
of a young
red-haired boy.

Six years-old,
no more,
he stands barefoot
before me
with a half-eaten muffin
in one hand,
wiping crumbs from lips
with the other.

The boy's face
is an open book
and looking
down
at his all too familiar chin
and nose
I find myself
reading between the lines.

From down the dark slip of corridor
a familiar voice
calls out
as lightning forks across the sky:

'Who is it Peter?'

'I don't know Daddy',
says the little boy.

Small feet
beat a retreat.

A light switch clicks.

The corridor dazzles
to life.

And then,
there he is,
my Dad —
standing
at the far end
of the corridor
with a baby
in his arms.

'Is that you, Pedro?
Is that you?'

Running from the truth

Legs pumping,

lungs burning,

I run
at full speed.

Witch-wood fingers
of needle green
reach out to grasp
my shirt,
my jeans,
my hair

as the storm clouds
cast their shadows

as the wind cackles
and moans;

but nothing
can slow me down
as I crash through
the forest's flaying hands.

Limbs pumping,

    lungs burning,

rain falling.

I run through branches

I run through the hurt

I run through disappointment

I tumble to the dirt.

The gift

Tied up in knots of anguish,
aching, sore and stiff
I lie beneath a Christmas tree —
                  a wet, unopened gift.

Gone forever

There is a pain that comes with knowing

and there is a pain

> *that comes with letting go.*

Sitting beneath this lonely pine
back to trunk,
knees
to chest,
I stare out
into this forest
of Christmas cheer
and cry.

Like Adam in the Garden of Eden

I feel naked
and exposed —

my soul stripped bare.

Reaching down,
I pick up
a handful
of damp pine needles
—leaves too thin
to ever cover up
my shame —
and watch them
as they drop back down
to the ground
through the cracks
in my fingers.

In my mind
I picture
the red-haired boy's face
and feel
my innocence
slipping away —
                    lost forever;

gone forever

like the girls I never kissed

the books I never read

and the mornings I never got out of bed.

Under a sheltering pine

As the worst of the rain
starts to ease,
I break open my journal
and write.

A stream of vile words
and self-pitying thoughts
spills out
onto the page:

black scratched accusations,

hot-blooded expletives,

lines of pure hate

and questions of "why me?"

My head
is full of weeds.

I fill three pages
with inky thistles
and vine choking lines
until I can finally
write
no more.

And that's when it comes to me
from the spent ashes of my anger
like a phoenix rising

two simple words,

"be alive".

Amongst all the weeds,
Johnny's words
lift off the page
as fresh as green sprouting shoots.

I look down
at those two
simple words
and shout them out
to the sky.

Feeling a little better,
I pick myself off the ground,
wipe the mud off my jeans
and start the long
lonely walk
back
into town.

The taste of apple

A motel room,
The Holiday Inn,
Colac.

Wet and dripping,
I step
from the bathroom,

    towel to waist,

and sit myself down
on the freshly made bed.

Dragging
the unopened present for Dad
onto my lap
I rip through
the rain-soaked wrapping paper
and reach inside the box,
pulling out a
big red apple.

The apple
is shiny-crisp
and as I lift
it to my lips
my stomach
growls.

I shove the apple
into my mouth
and bite down hard.

The apple cracks
and splits,
releasing
its richness —
sweet juice
that sluices
around my mouth

before slipping down
the back of my throat.

Every sugar crunch
feels good,
tastes good,
is good.

Ripe and rich,

this apple

was meant

to be eaten.

Forbidden fruit

Looking down
at the apple core
in the palm of my hand,
I think of Mr Santiago's words of wisdom,
instructing me to eat the apple
and finally
start to understand.

It's gotta be a riddle,
a figure of speech.

Adam.
The Garden of Eden.
The tree of knowledge.
    Forbidden fruit
and all that other religious stuff.

That's what Mr Santiago
was on about, wasn't it?

I toss the core
into my mouth
and chew through
the fibrous
remains.

I grind
everything up
into a pulp;
seeds and all.

'Ok Mr Santiago, you win,'
I say to myself, taking a deep breath.

It's good to harvest knowledge.

And it's good to know the truth
—even the hard to swallow kind.

Wiping the juice
from my lips,
I look down at the open box
full of apples,
full of knowledge
and try to remind myself that
unlike Adam
I haven't been thrown
out of the garden —
        the truth is,
that, despite the inescapable pain
I've busted back in.

I know who I am
and I know
where I belong.

I belong
to Mum;
to her bent knees
and whispered prayers.

I belong to
Evie's outstretched hand.

I belong
to Johnny's song,

I belong
to the snapping sound
of shears
on worn out wood.

My poem: Seeds of change

Underneath the slabs
of choking concrete
grass will drill its fingers
through the cracks.

Underneath the gossip
of Johnny's falling
memories of his voice
keep flooding back.

Underneath her prayers
and regulations
my mother's hands keep
reaching out to heal.

Underneath the ground
lies potential,
rising from the soil
our hopes revealed.

Underneath the smoke
sit the embers,
ready to ignite
and burst to flame.

Underneath the apple skin
there is knowledge
and hidden deep within
the seeds of change.

Appendix: Song and Spoken Word Lyrics

God bless the grass

God bless the grass that grows through the crack.
They roll the concrete over it to try and keep it back.
The concrete gets tired of what it has to do,
It breaks and it buckles and the grass grows thru,
And God bless the grass.

God bless the truth that fights toward the sun,
They roll the lies over it and think that it is done
It moves through the ground and reaches for the air,
And after a while it is growing everywhere,
And God bless the grass.

God bless the grass that breaks through cement,
It's green and its tender and it's easily bent,
But after a while it lifts up its head,
For the grass is living and the stone is dead.
And God bless the grass.

God bless the grass that's gentle and low
Its roots they are deep and its will is to grow.
And God bless the truth, the friend of the poor,
And the wild grass growing at the poor man's door,
And God bless the grass

– written by Malvina Reynolds

Johnny's song

Morning hangs like a veil
Our broken dreams fill these graves
Our prayers scratch holes in the sky
We came here to mourn, not to die

I reach for your hand as we walk
Your skin is so tense but so warm
Soldiers stand around with their guns
I'm drowning in screams as we run

I watch you fall
A lifeless bird from the sky
You slip through my fingers
No kiss, no goodbye

So I lay down – my arms around you
Shots fire while I cry for you,
for you

Wiping hair from your face
You stare, vacant eyes, into space
Sticky, wet, red are my hands
Your body lies limp in my arms

I watch you fall
A lifeless bird from the sky
You slip through my fingers
No kiss, no goodbye

So I lay down – my arms around you
Shots fire while I cry for you,
Mum, I miss you

Stone

Stone
Feelings frozen
Stone
Thoughts suffocating

He's not falling through my memories
He's not smashing through my dreams
His face is just a whisper
From a vague and distant scene

Stone
Feelings frozen
Stone
Thoughts suffocating

There's some lines of stone near Colac
Like the walls around my heart
Spinning me in circles
Forever to the start

'Waves of regret
Waves of joy
Did you reach out for the one you tried to destroy?'
Stone this feeling blocked and hardened
Nothing there
Oh, beg your pardon! Do I care, dare, stare?
Barren and bare
Tear, tear
But I can't, the stone
The solid stone
Lodged within these bones,
Groans
It groans.

Stone
Feelings frozen
Stone
Thoughts suffocating

He was stoned in clouds of blindness
Stoned for his uncle's sins
Can you see the ripples fading
From the stone that's fallen in?

Stone
Feelings frozen
Stone
Thoughts suffocating

Acknowledgements

Jacket Image and Design: Josh Durham

"God Bless the Grass", words & music by Malvina Reynolds, Copyright 1964 Schroder Music Co. (ASCAP). Renewed 1992, Used by permission. All rights reserved.

Many people have played a part in bringing this novel and audio CD to life.

We would like to thank in particular Clare Batten, Katherine Stewart and Peter Chapman for their endless support, advice, inspiration and assistance throughout this project.

Our gratitude is also extended to all the musicians who contributed their time and their talents in the production of the novel's audio tracks. These musicians include: Jack Senior, Gemma Belfrage, Luke McKenzie, Peter Slater, Finn Laidler, Isobel Stewart and Ewen Stewart.

Other individuals who deserve recognition and our appreciation include: Josh Durham for his magnificent cover design; and all the staff at IP for their work and support in the first publishing of this novel.